TOO LATE

"I'll ride my horse," Martha said. "He's already saddled. I don't want the Indians to get him."

Vern Wingate slapped the lines, and the team, though tired, broke into a choppy gallop.

"Let's get out of here," Wade said. "No sense in stretching our luck."

"I've got a box of keepsakes under my bed," Martha said suddenly. "I've got to save that."

Wade shook his head and followed Martha inside.

Martha was on her knees reaching under the bed for her box when Vern heard a sound that sent an icy chill down his back: the frenzied whoop of murder-bound Indians as they located another homestead to plunder.

Blood on the Prairie

Wayne C. Lee

LEISURE BOOKS NEW YORK CITY

A LEISURE BOOK®

May 2008

Published by special arrangement with Golden West Literary Agency.

Dorchester Publishing Co., Inc.
200 Madison Avenue
New York, NY 10016

ISBN 10: 0-8439-6099-X
ISBN 13: 978-0-8439-6099-0

Printed in the United States of America.

10 9 8 7 6 5 4 3 2 1

Visit us on the web at www.dorchesterpub.com.

Blood on the Prairie

I

Wade Harper came out on top of the bluff overlooking the Saline River just as the sun was withdrawing its fiery breath from the prarie. He reined in his horse to let him blow while he scanned the hills across the river.

For a year and a half he had trailed a man, and now he was near the end of that trail.

The final rays of the sun gave the grass a crimson hue that brought to Wade's mind the words of an old army scout he had met in Kansas City.

"The prairie will run red with blood before this summer is over," the old scout had said. "Mark my words. Those redskins are sweet as syrup on the outside, but they're mean as poison inside."

Wade urged his horse down the grassy slope of the bluff to the river. The river was hidden from the bluff by trees—cottonwood, elm, and a few ash and oak. Beyond the river the land rose again to the hills and plains, bare of everything but grass, as unattractive to anyone used to timber as a man's bald head.

But Wade had little thought for the bare hills. He had ridden across them most of the day. Back east somewhere, he had crossed the Solomon River. There had been trees there, too. But in between stretched miles of emptiness.

He rode cautiously through the trees to the river. Somewhere up there was the beginning of a town, an outpost in the civilization that was pushing into the land of the savage red man. It was toward this town that Wade was moving. But the threat of trouble and treachery that was uppermost in his mind did not come from men with red skins.

The talkative old scout he had met in Kansas City had come through that way less than a month ago, and a casual remark he had made about a man he had seen in the new town of Paradise had put Wade on his horse and caused him to head west.

"One of the biggest critters I ever seen wearing pants," the old scout had said. "A young fellow about thirty, I reckon, with straw hair. A foot taller than me, and he'd weigh more than a butchering hog."

To Wade, that could mean only one man: Herman Dack. Day after day, month after month, Wade had looked for this man along the fringe of civilization, shifting from one job to another, always on the move, searching for the big man who would stand out in any crowd.

Now he was certain he was nearing the end of his search. But the satisfaction he had savored was gone, and in its place was the brassy taste of defeat. He should have known that Dack would eventually get around to coming to Paradise, the town Wade's father had laid out. Jason Harper had believed in Dack when Dack served under him during the War between the States. And nobody had ever convinced Jason of the truth about the man.

His horse satisfied, Wade reined around and rode to the top of the bluff again. There was a road there, little more than a trail, and it ran west. It had to lead to Paradise. There was no other place for it to go.

Deep dusk was settling over the land as he put his horse to a canter. Perhaps it was just as well that he would come into Paradise in the dark. Then he could face Dack in the light of a new day.

A coyote somewhere off across the river lifted his voice in the early night, and Wade thought he heard a movement down in the trees not too far from the road. Perhaps it was a horse or a cow that had strayed from the town, which must be close now.

He thought of the rider he had seen off to his right early that morning as he was leaving Junction City. That rider had seemed in a big hurry, and he had been heading west. He had probably gone to Minneapolis, a town on the Solomon. If he hadn't, perhaps he was camping down along the river, and it was his horse that Wade had heard.

Every sound held its potential of danger. If Dack knew Wade was coming, he'd find some way of stopping him.

Wade kept all his senses alert as he followed the road that now swung to the left and began to dip down from the bluff toward the trees. The town of Paradise would be down there somewhere. The few letters he had received from his sister, Jennie, had described the town.

There was a quiet in the air as he rode into the trees that tightened his nerves to the breaking point. Even the crickets he had heard up on the prairie were silent here.

Then suddenly a man loomed up in front of Wade's horse as he rode into a heavy grove of cottonwoods. Even though he couldn't see well, Wade knew the man held a gun. His hand dropped to the butt of his own gun. But there it stopped as a voice behind him cut through the stillness:

"Keep your hands out in the clear."

Wade slowly spread his hands a foot to either side of him. He turned his head to look at the man behind him. This man was quite a bit taller than the one in front of him. But neither was Herman Dack. A third man appeared from the trees, even shorter and heavier than the man in front of Wade. If this was Dack's doing, he himself was keeping clear of it.

"Get down," the tall man said.

Wade got down without touching the saddle horn. He turned to face the tall man, sensing that he was the leader of the three. The first man who had appeared moved up behind him and lifted his gun from its holster.

"What's the idea?" Wade asked.

"Who invited you here?" the tall man asked.

"Since when does a man have to have an invitation

to ride where he pleases?"

Wade backed against his horse where he could see all three men. He knew the pattern; he had seen it before. The tall man was merely stalling with his questions. He didn't care what answer Wade gave. They had come to do a job, and they were just waiting for an opportunity to begin.

The tall man moved close, and Wade concentrated on him. It was a mistake. The shortest of the three suddenly lunged at him from the side. Wade wheeled and caught the man a heavy blow on the side of his face. Still he came on, his fists slowed but not stopped. Wade slammed another fist into the man's face, and he halted like a runaway wagon against a stone wall.

But the other two were in it now. A sharp pain shot through Wade's head as a fist connected with his ear. He lashed out with both fists and brought up a knee, catching the tall man in the side. It spun him around, and Wade threw all his weight behind a punch aimed at the man's nose. It connected, and the blood spurted.

But the short fellow was in motion again, and his fists were the most telling of any. He was a younger man, Wade guessed, for there was terrific power in his short arms and legs.

A blow caught Wade in the stomach, and he doubled over involuntarily. Another fist straightened him up, and he lashed out blindly, trying desperately to punish as much as he was being punished and knowing he had no chance of doing it.

He felt blood dripping from his chin and tasted it in his mouth. Fists were pounding him from every side. He was dragged away from his horse, and now he had no protection from behind. Still he refused to go down. He knew a moment of vague satisfaction when he gave one of the men a solid blow to the chin, and the latter reeled backward and went down.

But in a moment that satisfaction was gone. A blow on the ear and another on the chin sent lights flashing before his eyes. He reeled back, feeling for his horse. But the horse was gone. Then another fist caught up with him and clubbed him to the ground.

He tried to get up, but his legs refused. Each second he expected a kick in the side or a boot in the face. But there was nothing, and he relaxed, letting numbness ease the pain that racked him.

He didn't lose consciousness, but his mind was in a fog. When it cleared, he remained motionless, for he was aware that the men had not left.

"Ain't he come to yet?" one man growled.

The shortest man moved closer, a squat man built like a cottonwood stump. Wade, watching through nearly closed eyes, could testify that he could move like a cat.

"He's playing 'possum,'" the man said, and thumped a toe into Wade's ribs.

Wade flinched in spite of himself, and the tall man reached down and clutched a handful of Wade's bloody shirt front.

"Listen and listen good," the man said. "You're not wanted here. This is just a sample of what you'll get if you're not long gone from here by morning."

The man released his hold, and Wade dropped back on the ground. He didn't see the short fellow moving in again until his pointed boot toe punched into his side.

"Just a sample," the man repeated.

Wade made a feeble pass at the boot, hoping to catch it. But the man backed out of his reach. Wade stared at the big bulk in the dim light. He'd remember that shape even though he couldn't see the man's face. He'd never forget.

"Some day—" he panted.

"There won't be any some day," the short man

snapped, and slammed his boot into Wade's ribs again. Pain shot through Wade's side and he held his breath, anticipating the next kick. But the tall man caught the short fellow's arm and pulled him away.

"Don't cripple him so he can't ride," the tall man said. "I think he understands now. Come on."

The three men disappeared like shadows, and a minute later, Wade heard horses walking away. He sank back and let the fog close in over him. . . .

Cold water splashing in his face brought him back to consciousness with a jolt. He tried to sit up but sank back with a groan. Through a haze he made out a small man bending over him.

"Able to move?" the man asked softly.

Wade groaned. "I reckon. Are you here to make sure I get out of the country?"

The man crouched beside Wade, still speaking softly. "My name is Solly Ingram. I'm a minister."

Wade raised himself to one elbow. "I don't need a preacher yet. But I could sure use a doc."

"Paradise has no doctor," Ingram said. "I came to help you."

Wade shook his head, trying to clear it. "How come you knew I was here or that I needed help?"

Solly Ingram shook out his hat, which he had used to carry water up from the river. "I'm a little fellow, but I've got mighty big ears. Sandy Spurlock—he was the tall fellow that helped work you over—was in Junction City last night. He found out who you were and figured you'd come here, I reckon. He came dashing into town late this afternoon like Jehu without his chariot. I smelled trouble, and when he rode out here with Bradley and Ardy Orr, I followed."

"Now you're going to help me get on my horse and head back toward Junction City?"

Ingram scratched his head. "Doesn't look to me like you're in any shape to ride far tonight. Anyway, you don't strike me as the running kind. You stood up to those jackals like a Daniel. And believe me, Paradise could use a Daniel. I live in a house at the very end of town. Nobody bothers me. I reckon you can stay there for a few days till you pull yourself together."

"What about my horse?" Wade asked. "They'll find it and know I'm still around."

"There's a barn with plenty of hay where I keep my horse right behind my house. My place belonged to a farmer who moved away in a hurry. Your father brought him in when he first started the town."

"You know who I am?" Wade asked in surprise.

"I heard Spurlock drop the name when he rode in. I guessed your name was what lit the fire under him."

Wade got to his feet slowly, the pain in his side like the stab of a knife. "If you've got a place to tuck me away for a day or two, preacher, I'll take it."

"I'll get your horse," Solly Ingram said, and disappeared into the trees.

II

A sharp pain in his side brought Wade back to the land of reality. He started up, then sank back with a groan. Light filled the room, and he realized the night was gone. Solly Ingram was standing by the bed.

"Guess I prodded a little hard," the preacher said. "I wanted to find out if anything was broken."

"Well," Wade said, breathing hard, "is there?"

"Don't think so," Ingram said. "But you've sure got a nasty bruise on your side. Won't take too long to heal, though, if the ribs aren't cracked."

"I know who did that," Wade said as the sharp pain faded, leaving only a dull ache. "I got a look at his shape. Like a barrel."

"That was Ardy Orr," Ingram said, "Bradley Orr's boy. They run a blacksmith shop down the street."

Wade sat up on the bed. "Who's this Spurlock you mentioned last night?"

Ingram went into the other room and came back with a pot of coffee. "Here. Take a swig of this. I didn't figure you'd remember anything I said last night. Sandy Spurlock runs the new hotel and saloon here in Paradise."

"One of Dack's men?" Wade asked, taking the cup of hot coffee Ingram handed him.

"What do you know about Dack?" Ingram asked sharply.

"As much as anybody in this town. I've been hunting him for a year and a half. What's your opinion of him? He's here, isn't he?"

Ingram pulled a chair around and sat down, pouring himself a cup of coffee. "He's here, all right," he said slowly. "But what I think of him doesn't seem to agree with anyone else's opinion."

"Which tells me nothing," Wade said when the preacher paused.

"I could be wrong," Ingram said. "I don't like to condemn a man without good cause. But I pride myself on being able to see into the souls of men. I don't like all I see in Herman Dack."

"You're seeing him right then," Wade said. "Nobody else agrees with you?"

Ingram shook his head. "They see only the gentleman who walks down the street like he owned it. And in a way, he does."

Wade leaned forward, ignoring the pain in his side. "What do you mean by that?"

The preacher shifted uncomfortably. "I've talked too much already. I'm not saying there isn't a lot of good in Herman Dack. I'm sure there is. He claims he is doing the town a service by letting certain fighting men move in. Maybe he is. I don't know. But I do know a lot of good men have left, including the man who owned this house. A lot of others just like him have left, especially the farmers close to town. Am I making sense?"

Wade nodded. "Just as much as if you were reading out of your Bible. I suppose Dad worships Dack and everything he does?"

Ingram nodded. "That's how he got such a grip on things so quick. This was Jason Harper's town. He laid it out and coaxed people to come here. He called it Paradise because he thought it was just that. Then Dack came, followed by Spurlock and the Orrs. It isn't paradise any more." Ingram got up. "I'll fix you some breakfast."

Wade watched him go into the other room and heard things rattling on the stove. He realized how hungry he was. He hadn't eaten anything but some cold biscuits and meat since early yesterday morning in Junction City.

The smell of frying bacon drifted in from the other room, and Wade's hunger grew. The sizzling stopped, and a minute later Solly Ingram brought in a plate heaped with bacon and eggs.

"This ought to stall you for a while," he said, and set the plate down. Then he pulled up his chair and leaned forward. "If you don't mind talking, I'd like to know just what you've got against Dack."

Wade bit into a slice of bacon.

"Two years ago, in the spring of '66, Dad came out here from Indiana where we lived," he said. "I didn't want to come, so I stayed there and took over the store Dad had. I had a partner, another war veteran about five years older than me.

"Dack showed up that summer. I knew him pretty well. I served in the cavalry with him for nearly three years, having joined up when I was seventeen. My partner's wife was as pretty a woman as you'll ever see. I knew what a woman chaser Dack was. But I couldn't convince my partner even when Dack started mooning around his wife.

"Well, Dack ran off with her. My partner went to pieces, finally took after Dack and was found dead in Kansas City. No proof that Dack killed him. But the way I see it, he killed him whether he pulled the trigger or not."

"What happened to your partner's wife? Dack has no woman here."

"He dropped her like he drops every woman after he's had her for a while. I saw her in a little town in Iowa. She was so ashamed she wouldn't even talk to me. Our business wasn't too prosperous, anyway, and when that scandal hit us, we went broke. I took to the trails, looking for Dack. I've got more than just that score to settle with him. Beside, what he's done before, he'll do again if he isn't stopped."

"And you figure on stopping him?" Ingram asked, rubbing his chin thoughtfully.

"Know of anybody with a better reason—or a better chance? Remember, I've got my sister, Jennie, to think of."

Ingram nodded. "Reason enough, I reckon. But patience can be your greatest virtue. Dack is a popular man here, well liked. He knew you were coming here and he probably knew why. When he finds out you're still here—"

"I'll take my chances," Wade said. "I have to."

"Dack is a big fellow, rough and ready," Ingram said. "But he has never stooped to anything beneath the dignity of a gentleman. And he has a charm for women that is hard to understand. I'm afraid your sister is no exception."

"I'm going to talk to Dad and Jennie right away," Wade said.

Ingram was on his feet in an instant. "You're going to stay right here today," he said sharply. "The minute you step onto the street, you're a marked man. And you're in no shape for trouble yet. I've got some linament I bought to use on my horse a while back. I don't see that there is much difference in the muscles of a horse or a man. I'll get it."

Wade saw the wisdom of the preacher's advice, and he settled back to wait in spite of the impatience gnawing at him.

Wade fretted away three days in Solly's house. The

pain in his side disappeared, and the bruises on his face faded to dark blotches. He resolved to wait no longer.

Solly came in at sundown, loaded down with things from the store. "You've got a smart sister, Wade," he said. "She got curious about all the grub I've been buying. So I told her you were here. I said you'd be up to see her and your folks tonight."

"About time you let me out of this jail," Wade said.

It was dark by the time supper was over. Wade buckled on his gun and stepped out into the street, getting his first look at the town his father had laid out. The street ran east and west, Ingram's house being the last house on the west end. There were no lights on the street, but Wade had no trouble making out the buildings as he walked past them. His father's store was the next to last building at the east end of the street, Solly had said.

Wade went past three or four houses, all but one built of logs. That one was sod. Then he came to a long low building that ran back almost into the hill. A sign swinging in the light breeze declared it to be the Blacksmith. This would be the Orrs' business. Then there was the saloon that connected with the only two-story building in town, the hotel.

All the buildings were on the north side of the street, backed against the bluff, facing the river. Wade walked on, noting that the only horses on the street were two tied in front of the saloon. It was quiet, even the noise from the saloon not drowning out the murmur of the river that ran through the trees on Wade's right.

Then he came to the store. The front part of it was dark, but there was a light in the back. Jennie's letters had said they were living in the back of the store building. Wade went to the back door and rapped.

His welcome was a hearty one. Neglected threads of family ties were picked up. But Wade avoided the question of why he had come to Paradise. He'd save that explanation until he could talk to Jason alone. That chance came later in the evening when Wade's mother and sister had gone to bed.

"Now that all the fuss is over," Jason Harper said, settling back in his chair, "let's get down to facts. You didn't come to Paradise just for a visit."

Wade studied his father's stern face.

"You're right; I didn't come for a visit," he said. "I came mostly to protect Jennie."

Jason frowned. "Jennie? She's safe enough here; as

safe, anyway, as anyone can be on these plains with the unrest among the Indians."

"I wasn't thinking of the Indians," Wade said. "Why did you take Herman Dack in as partner in your store?"

"He makes a good partner," Jason said, his back becoming ramrod stiff.

"Herman Dack ran off with the wife of my partner back in the store in Indiana, then killed the man when he trailed Dack to Kansas City. I don't expect you to believe that. But that's the kind of a man you're letting hang around Jennie."

"Herman wouldn't harm a hair of Jennie's head," Jason said, never blinking an eye. "I have complete faith in him. And so has everyone else. He wanted to be a partner in my store so that he can build a reputation. Some day, when this Indian fighting is over, Kansas will be a great state. And Herman Dack will be an important man in the state. I'll do my part to boost him to that position."

Wade nodded. "I suppose you will, unless somebody kills him first. Why did he bring in men like Spurlock and the Orrs?"

"He didn't bring them in," Jason said, a little calmer

now. "They just came. They're rough men, but we need such men while this frontier is so unsettled."

"What about the men you coaxed into coming here and Dack has run out?"

He hasn't run anybody out," Jason said, his voice rising again. "They have just been leaving. With all the Indian unrest, you can't blame them too much. The men I brought here were farmers with families, not fighting men. Herman goes to Junction City, Topeka, even Kansas City, every so often to try to convince the right kind of people to come here and settle. We need fighting men here now. When the Indians have been subdued, then the farmer will come back."

Wade saw that he could do nothing to change Jason's mind. He turned toward the door.

"Where are you going?" Jason demanded.

"Back to Solly Ingram's. I've been staying there since he brought me in after the beating Dack's 'fine' men gave me the night I rode in."

"You're welcome to stay here. I never turned one of my children away from my own bed and board."

"I may come back tomorrow to stay," Wade said. "But I'm going back to Solly's tonight."

III

The next morning after breakfast, Wade put on his hat and headed for the door. "I think it's time I had a talk with Dack," he told Solly.

"Watch your step. You won't be winning any popularity contest in town if you lock horns with Dack."

Wade went out into the street. Dack, he figured, would be in the store this morning.

The blacksmith shop was open and a young man was leaning in the doorway. Wade would have recognized that shape even if Solly hadn't described him. He was directly under the sign that read "Blacksmith—Bradley and Ardon Orr, Props." He looked more Indian than white, Wade thought. His skin was dark, almost bronze, and his cheek bones were high. He also had the straight black hair and black eyes of an Indian; according to

Solly, his mother was a Cheyenne.

There was no expression on his face as Wade walked past. If he was surprised to see that Wade was still there, he didn't let it show. When Wade reached the porch of the hotel, he looked back. Ardy Orr was still there, and his father was with him now, both looking after Wade.

Wade would have gone on past the hotel toward the store if the door hadn't opened just then. A big man stepped out, blocking Wade's path.

"Well, what do you know? My old cavalry buddy."

Wade sized up Herman Dack. He hadn't changed a bit, as far as he could see. His six foot six inch frame had carried about two hundred and forty pounds when Wade had seen him last. It still did. He had the same fixed smile on his handsome face, and he wore his clothes in the same careless way.

Wade saw only one unusual thing about him—the ring with the huge sparkling stone that couldn't escape notice. Wade knew little about gems, but he was sure that it was a diamond. He wondered how Dack had come by it. Wade had never known Dack to have enough money for a ring like that.

"What are you doing here, Wade?" Dack asked as

if Wade's appearance were a complete surprise to him.

"I came to find out what you are doing here," Wade said.

"I'll tell you; then you can go back where you came from," Dack said, the smile on his face never changing. "I'm a partner in the captain's store, and I'm helping build a community that will some day be the bright spot of the state."

"And you figure to be the big wheel here," Wade said.

Dack's grin widened a little. "You don't doubt that, do you? Kansas is going to be a great state. No reason why Paradise shouldn't supply one of its best men."

The door of the store down the street suddenly burst open, and a squarely built man stamped onto the porch. He went directly to a buckboard standing at the hitch-rack and took a rifle off the seat. A girl ran after him, catching his arm, but he pushed her aside and strode toward the hotel.

For a moment, Wade wondered if the man was coming for Dack. But Dack only watched, unconcerned. Then the man stopped and yelled:

"Hey, Spurlock. Come on out and fight like a man."

Dack moved then, stepping off the hotel porch and

going out to meet the man. "Take it easy, Wingate," he said. "You don't want to tangle with Sandy. You're no gunman."

"He's trying to steal my land," Wingate said. "No man living can do that."

"What will happen to your wife and daughter if Sandy kills you?"

Wingate's determination faltered. His eyes shifted from the hotel door to Dack, then down to the rifle in his hand. Evidently Dack had struck a tender spot.

Sandy Spurlock came out on the porch of the hotel and stopped just a few feet from Wade, his steel gray eyes on Wingate.

"Somebody call me?"

Wade measured the man quickly. In spite of his almost white hair, he appeared to be in his early thirties; a gambler, judging from his dress and the soft whiteness of his face and hands. There was a dark bruise under one eye. Wade was pretty sure he knew how that bruise had gotten there. He looked at the way Spurlock wore his gun and the steadiness of the hand hovering close to the butt of that gun. Dack was right. No ordinary farmer such as Wingate had any business tangling with a man like Spurlock.

"It's all right, Sandy," Dack said smoothly. "Wingate just got a little mixed up."

"I'll be happy to straighten him out," Spurlock said softly.

Dack spoke sharply. "I said it was all right. Go on back inside."

Spurlock hesitated a moment longer, then turned and went silently into the hotel. If there had been the slightest doubt in Wade's mind that Spurlock was Dack's hired gun, it was gone now.

Wade strode on down the street, watching Wingate turn back toward the buckboard, the barrel of his rifle brushing the dust at his plodding feet. Jennie had come out of the store and joined the girl who had tried to stop Wingate.

"Oh, Wade," Jennie called to him, "I want you to meet a good friend of mine, Martha Wingate. She and her folks live on a homestead northwest of town."

Wade took a good look at Martha Wingate as he moved toward the two girls. She was about eighteen, Jennie's age, or maybe a trifle older, about an inch taller and just as slim. But there the resemblance ended. She didn't have the blunt chin that both Jennie and Wade had. Her features were rather small and delicate, but there was strength and pride in her black eyes.

She was fighting back tears now, and Wade realized that Jennie had called him over to introduce him mainly to get Martha's mind off the near tragedy they had just witnessed.

"I'm glad to meet any friend of Jennie's," he said.

Martha dabbed at her eyes. "If it wasn't for Jennie, I'd be ready to give up and get out."

"Apparently somebody is trying to get you to do just that," Wade said.

"Sandy Spurlock is trying to buy our place, just like he bought all the others around here."

Wade frowned. Was Spurlock that wealthy? Or was he buying for Dack? If so, where had Dack gotten the money?

"Has your father proved up so he can sign over a deed?" Wade pressed.

"Sandy doesn't want the land," Martha said bitterly. "He just wants us gone."

"Sandy has put other men on some of the farms he bought," Jennie volunteered. "He gets the original owners to sign the land across somehow. I don't understand it all. But the Wingates are not leaving!"

Wingate came from the buckboard, his face flushed

with suppressed rage and shame.

"If that man ever comes on my place again," he said heavily, "I'll kill him, so help me, if I have to shoot him in the back."

Wade thought he suddenly saw a light. Dack and Spurlock had a reason for wanting Wingate out of the country. He might not be much of a fighter or a particularly brave man. But he was a dangerous one if crowded far enough. And apparently he had been crowded to that extent.

A rider appeared at the east end of the street, and the sight of the lathered horse and his excited rider drove all other considerations into the background.

The man yanked his horse to a stop at the first hitch-rack in front of the store. Jason Harper came running out of the store and reached the man ahead of the others coming down the street.

"What's wrong, Sam?" Jason demanded.

"There's been an Indian raid on Council Grove," the man panted, sliding out of his saddle.

A deathly silence greeted the news. Wade glanced over the men and women who had gathered at sight of the frightened man. There was fear on almost every face.

"When did it happen?" Jason finally asked.

"The fifth of June, they told me in Junction City," the messenger said.

"That's almost a week ago," Sandy Spurlock exclaimed.

"We could have been wiped out before we had any idea the redskins were on the warpath," Wingate said, more awe than fear in his voice.

Wingate was standing only a few feet from Spurlock, but neither man had any thought for the other now.

Wade didn't know too much about the geography of Kansas, but he did know that Council Grove was south and a little east of Junction City. That meant it was south and at least eighty miles east of Paradise. If the Indians could strike at a settlement the size of Council Grove that far to the east, they could do about as they pleased with an isolated little place like Paradise. Wade guessed that several of those around him were thinking the same.

Herman Dack, towering over the other men, moved up to the messenger. "Now, Sam, tell us all you know. How many were killed? What tribe of Indians?"

"I don't know how many were killed," Sam said. "They told me it was Tall Bull that led the raid."

"Cheyenne," Dack said quickly. "Any reason why they picked Council Grove?"

"They said they were really raiding the Kaw Indians. Stole all their horses."

Jason Harper let his breath out in a long sigh. "Maybe they weren't raiding the whites, after all," he said. "The Indian tribes are always fighting with each other."

"Just why did they want the Kaw horses?" Wade asked.

Solly Ingram had come from his house at the far end of the street. Now he spoke up. "There are only two times when Indians need extra horses: when they go on a hunt or on the warpath."

"I say it's time we all got back east where we're safe," Sam, the messenger, said.

"Now wait a minute," Dack put in quickly. "These raids happen among the Indian tribes all the time. Just because this one took place close to us and some white people were involved is no reason for us to lose our heads. Let's hold a meeting and talk it over. We can plan some sort of defense."

"What defense is there against a thousand murdering redskins?" Sam grumbled.

But Dack's suggestion met with general approval,

and a meeting was set for that night in Spurlock's saloon, the only building in town with a room large enough to hold more than a dozen people. Wingate promised to let the farmers north and west of town know about the meeting, and Sam, who farmed just east of town, said he'd let the others know.

"Think everybody will leave?" Wade asked Solly as the little knot of people in front of the store broke up.

"Some may," Solly said. "But most will stay. Dack, you noticed, didn't panic. He'll talk most of them into staying. He's mighty smooth with words. In David's words, he has a 'deceitful tongue.' "

Wade went to the meeting, uncertain how things would go. Jason Harper, recognized as the leader, called the meeting to order. But Wade noticed that within five minutes, Herman Dack was on the floor and in charge of proceedings. And Jason Harper didn't seem to resent it at all.

"We're as jumpy as a spooky horse in dry weeds," Dack said. "When one Indian tribe raids another, that doesn't mean any trouble for the whites. When two tribes get together and stage a war dance, then that's the time for whites to worry. I think we'd be foolish to leave here just because of the Cheyenne raid on the

Kaws."

Bradley Orr stood up. "He's right. I've lived with the Cheyennes for several years. I know them. When they get ready to make war on the whites, they either join up with other tribes or let them completely alone. They don't start a war with them."

Wade glanced at Solly. Would people believe a squaw man with a half-breed son?

A farmer from northeast of town stood up, not completely convinced that Orr was right in saying the Cheyennes meant no harm to the whites.

"I was in Minneapolis last week, and I heard there about a settler west of Delphos who got raided by Indians. Cheyennes, they figured. The man and his small boy had enough arrows in them to fill a bucket. Both were scalped and their fingers were torn off. Even worse happened to the man's wife."

An audible gasp came from the women present, and the faces of the men paled and drew tight.

"Stories like that grow with the telling," Dack said. "Maybe it's true; maybe it isn't. We all knew there were Indians here when we came. And these Indians aren't all friendly. If, at the first sign of alarm, we all gather here in town, we can defend ourselves, I'm sure."

Heads began to nod in agreement, and when Dack had finished his arguments five minutes later, the meeting broke up with each man determined to hang onto what he had hewn out of the prairie so far.

IV

It was almost eleven when Wade left his family an evening a week after his arrival to go back to Solly's. The late hour made the light in the blacksmith shop strike him as unusual. Instead of thumping across the porch of the hotel and saloon, he swerved out into the street and moved silently past the two-story building toward the blacksmith shop.

There he turned toward the bluff and ducked into the shadows between the blacksmith's and the saloon.

There was a small window in the side of the smithy just above the big anvil, and Wade headed for it, stumbling over a piece of iron that evidently had been discarded by the blacksmith. Though the window was up almost under the eaves, the building had a low roof and Wade could reach it without stretching.

He was disappointed, however. There was no glass in the window; just an opening to let in light and cool air. Tonight somebody had hung a thin cloth over the opening. The light from the lantern hanging on the pole in the center of the big room managed to seep out into the night, but Wade could see in only when a puff of the night breeze fluttered the cloth.

He caught just a glimpse of the men gathered close to the lantern once when the cloth flipped out for a moment. He couldn't be positive what he had seen. But he thought there were three men. Two were Bradley and Ardy Orr and the other, he was sure, was an Indian. Wade waited breathlessly for the wind to push the cloth aside so he could get another look. Next time he would be looking at that third man.

But a step behind him jerked his attention away from the window. He wheeled in time to catch a fist on the side of his head that must have been intended to strike the back of his neck and put him out.

In a flash Wade saw what had happened. The side door of the saloon was open now. Sandy Spurlock in the saloon must have heard him when he stumbled over the iron. Spurlock was crowding in on him now.

This time was different from the night when Wade

had first encountered Spurlock. Spurlock was alone now, and he didn't have the advantage of holding Wade under a gun until he was ready to begin the battle.

Wade drove into Spurlock, slamming a fist into his stomach and following with a blow to the face. Spurlock reeled back, his white hair spilling into his eyes. But he wasn't finished. He caught himself against the wall of the saloon and propelled himself forward like an angry bull.

Wade tried to sidestep but only partially escaped the charge. Both men went down, Wade on the bottom. Spurlock gouged and prodded with short jabs until Wade wiggled free and rolled to his feet. He knew he had to finish fast, for they were making a lot of noise. It would be only a matter of seconds before Bradley and Ardy Orr would be there to help Spurlock.

Spurlock was just getting to his feet when Wade got squared away. The moment Spurlock straightened, Wade was on him. He drove him back against the saloon wall and hammered his face and chest. Spurlock pushed away from the wall again and tried to crowd into Wade. But Wade had the upper hand now, and slowly Spurlock backed off until he was against the wall again.

Another few blows and Wade knew he would have the battle won. But time ran out on him. He heard footsteps behind him just before the weight of a huge man struck him. He bent double, and the man scooted over his shoulder. Then he wheeled to meet the charge of the second man.

The odds were the same now as they had been that first night out in the cottonwood grove. And Wade knew the result would be the same unless he got away. He wheeled toward the street, but a hand reached out and caught his foot. He went down with a heavy crash.

Instinctively he rolled to one side just in time to avoid the crushing weight of Ardy Orr, who had lunged full length at him. He scrambled to his feet, but Bradley Orr slammed into him, knocking him down again. Spurlock was reeling toward him now, intent on getting in on the kill.

Wade tried to roll away, but Bradley held him. Wade saw Ardy, on his feet again, aiming a heavy boot at his head. Wade jerked sideways, hoping to avoid the boot.

Right then a sharp voice cut through the gloom, suspending all action.

"Hold still, all of you. Bring that boot down, Ardy,

and it will be the last move you'll ever make."

Wade rolled to his feet. He recognized Solly Ingram's voice, and when he looked, he saw the faint metallic glint of starlight on steel. Solly had a gun. There was no doubting that he would use it, either. His voice had no quaver or hesitation in it.

"You're a little out of place, ain't you, Preacher?" Bradley Orr growled.

"I don't like to see a man beaten to death," Solly said quietly. "Come on, Wade."

"He was spying," Spurlock panted, leaning against the saloon wall. "I jumped him. Didn't even know who it was then."

"Still no reason for beating him to death," Solly said, and backed into the street, Wade moving beside him.

The three men made no attempt to follow, and Wade and Solly reached home without seeing them again.

Wade wore his gun carefully the next day when he went on the street. Sandy Spurlock had a reason to kill him now, as much reason as any gunman needed.

Wade stopped short on the porch of the saloon on his way to the store, for Spurlock had come out of the hotel ahead of him. This was it, Wade thought. Spurlock's face was puffed and blotched, but there was a grin of sorts threading its way between the bruises.

"No hard feelings about last night?" Spurlock asked.

Wade hesitated. "Should there be?"

"I can't see why. If I'd known who it was I might not have been so hasty about jumping you. But, after all, a fellow is mighty suspicious of a spy."

Wade nodded, letting Spurlock ramble on. He had something in mind, and Wade was willing to let him work his way around to it.

"I like the way you put up a scrap," Spurlock went on. "I could use you here in my business. You don't have a job. Surely you could use some money."

Wade frowned slightly. "I suppose I could. Just what are you driving at?"

"I'm running the hotel and saloon myself. There are times when I could use a little help, particularly if some fellow gets out of hand. After what I saw last night, I figure you're just the fellow to handle that job. You can take care of yourself."

"Evenings would be the only time you'd need me?" Wade asked.

Spurlock nodded. "I reckon. Oh, there might be an occasional day job. But you'll get well paid for any work you do."

Wade nodded. "It's a deal."

V

On the way back to Solly's place, Wade was hailed by Spurlock.

"Got a job for me already?" Wade asked cautiously.

"How did you know?"

"I don't figure you called me over just to be friendly."

"I've got an errand for you to run," Spurlock said with growing confidence. "You saw the run-in Vern Wingate and I had the other day."

Wade nodded.

"If Wingate stays in this country, we're going to meet out in the street some day. Now I'm not afraid of him. I know I'm faster with a gun than any clodhopper. But I don't like killing, and I want to avoid it if I can."

Wade began to understand. "And you want somebody to convince Wingate to get out of the country while he is still alive."

"Exactly," Spurlock said, trying to pull his bruised face into a grin. "I figure you're the one to do it. The Wingates think the Harpers are cut from good cloth. It might save a killing if you succeed."

Spurlock made it sound like good sense for Wingate to leave.

"I'll give it a try," Wade said. "But I gathered the other day that Wingate might be a little hard to convince."

"You can do it," Spurlock said.

It was almost noon, so Wade waited until after dinner, then saddled his horse and, following Solly's directions, rode out to the Wingate farm. It wasn't much of a place: just three sod buildings, a house, a barn and a chicken house. But there was a garden growing behind the house, and a few flowers were budding in the front yard.

Wade dismounted and started toward the door. Martha opened it.

"We weren't expecting visitors," she said. "Come in."

"Your father in the field?" Wade asked.

"No," Martha said. "He finished cultivating his corn this morning. He's patching some harness this afternoon. You'll find him in the barn."

Wade's eyes lingered a moment longer on Martha in her gingham dress and white dust cap before turning to the barn. He would much rather have accepted Martha's invitation into the house. But he had come to talk to Vern Wingate, and business came first.

Wingate's welcome was a hearty one. The only other time Wade had seen Wingate was on the day he had challenged Spurlock. He had been angry and ashamed that day. Now he was neither, and Wade found he liked the man.

"How does your corn crop look?" Wade asked.

"It's got a good chance if we get enough rain," Wingate said, "and if the redskins leave us alone."

"Don't you think it would be safer for you and your whole family somewhere else till the Indians settle down?"

Wingate nodded. "Sure, it would be safer. But we didn't come out here to be safe. We came to build a home. When the Indians have finally settled down, which will happen soon, we'll have a fine farm already going."

"What about your wife and Martha?"

A frown crossed Wingate's face. "Maybe you think I don't worry about them. But they're more determined than I am to stay right here. If anything happened to either one of them—" He twisted the leather in his hands until it squeaked.

"It's none of my business, I guess," Wade said, "but I'm curious about the trouble between you and Sandy Spurlock."

Wingate stared at Wade for a moment. "You're right: it isn't any of your business. But I don't mind telling you. Spurlock has been buying out the farmers all around, especially those right close to town. He's moved in his own breed of cats on some of the farms. I figure he's trying to build up a regular empire for himself."

"Is that all you've got against Spurlock?" Wade pressed. "Surely you wouldn't try to kill a man just because he wanted to buy your farm."

"It isn't all," Wingate growled, and jammed a hole in a broken strap where he was going to make a splice. "Spurlock has been playing up to Martha. As long as she didn't say anything, I didn't either, though I'd have liked it better if she'd kept a pet skunk around. But when she told Spurlock to get and he still hung around, I figured it was time for me to take a hand."

Wade nodded, getting a grasp on his racing thoughts. "Martha doesn't want him around now?"

"I don't think she ever did. Can't fool my Martha about a bad egg like that. She was just too polite to tell him to light out until he got too persistent. If he keeps pestering her, I'll have to do something."

Wade began to see things a lot more clearly than he had when he had ridden out.

"I need a drink of water," Wingate said, coming to the door behind Wade. "Let's go in the house."

Wade nodded agreement and followed Wingate across the yard. Before they reached the house, another rider loomed up over the knoll to the east. Wade recognized the huge frame of Herman Dack. Probably coming out to check on his progress, Wade thought.

Wingate waited and invited Dack into the house, too. The three went in, and Wade watched Martha closely to see her reaction to Dack. It was about as he had expected. She looked up to him with the respect due the kingpin in the community.

"You've got a mighty comfortable home here," Dack

said, relaxing in a chair. "I can see why Sandy is so set on buying you out." Idly he turned the diamond ring on his finger.

"He's not buying me out," Wingate said.

"Oh, I didn't say he's going to succeed," Dack said smoothly. "But I heard him say he'd like to own this place. He might even hire someone to run his hotel and saloon and live out here himself."

Vern Wingate snorted. "It will be a longer day than he's ever seen when he gets his thieving hands on this place."

"Good for you," Dack said heartily. "This country needs men with backbone like yours."

Wade saw the satisfaction that touched the Wingate family at Dack's praise. Dack was playing it safe. If anything happened to Wingate, he certainly wouldn't be blamed for it.

"I wish Sandy wasn't so set on getting this farm," Dack went on after a minute. "I'll talk to him and try to persuade him to get the idea out of his head. But he's a stubborn man. I'm not sure I can do anything."

"We'll appreciate anything you can do," Wingate said.

"And if I can't do anything, what will you do?"

Dack turned to look at Wade. "What would you suggest?"

Wade was slow in answering.

"A man has a right to his home," he said finally. "It's a free country; at least it's supposed to be. If this was my place and I wanted to live here, I'd tell Sandy Spurlock to go jump in the creek."

The last doubt faded from Wingate's face, and Martha smiled appreciatively at Wade.

Wade rose to leave, and Dack made an excuse to leave, too. They rode away from the farm together.

VI

The first night Wade showed up at the saloon for work, Spurlock fired him. Apparently Wade had been hired for the job of boosting Wingate out of the country and thus aligning himself with Spurlock in the eyes of the town. When he didn't fall for that bait Spurlock wanted nothing more to do with him.

Wade took his saddled horse up to the store late one afternoon. He had to talk to Jennie, and the open prairie was the most private place for that. He expected to find Dack in the store ready to object to Wade taking his own sister for a ride on the praire. But Dack wasn't there.

"He went to Topeka and he might go on to Kansas City," Jennie said when Wade asked. "He makes that trip every once in a while, looking for more settlers who will come and help us build up a strong community here."

"Does he bring back many?" Wade asked, toying with a coffee grinder on the counter.

Jennie shook her head. "He hasn't had much luck. But he keeps trying. He's doing a lot for Paradise."

Wade nodded. "How about taking a ride, Jennie? It's nice out."

"I'd love it," she said, whipping off her apron. "I don't get to ride much. Daddy says it isn't safe to ride alone, with the Indians so unsettled. And Herman doesn't take me riding very often."

"Dad's right. It certainly isn't safe for a girl to ride alone. I'm surprised Vern Wingate lets Martha come to town alone."

"I guess they feel safer out there than we do here in town. Saddle my horse for me, Wade."

The sun was less than half an hour high when Wade and Jennie rode out of town and up the bluff to the level of the prairie. In a swale half a mile from town, Wade stopped and loosened the rein on his horse so that he could crop the grass that stood halfway to his knees. Jennie followed Wade's example.

"You've got something on your mind, haven't you,

Wade?" Jennie said.

Wade nodded. "I have had ever since I came here and found Herman Dack. You know what I think of him, so we won't go into that. But I want to ask you some things."

Jennie was obviously on the defensive. "What?"

"Do you really think Dack is trying to help Dad's business and the town?"

"I know he is," Jennie said quickly. "Look how he has fixed up the store. Some lumber for a better front is all we need now to have a nice-looking place. And look how he's working to bring in people to settle the community. That will build up the town and also make us safer from the Indians."

"Ever question the kind of people he's bringing in?" Wade asked.

"He's bringing in fighting men," Jennie said without hesitation. "That's what we have to have until the Indians are quieted down. Most of the farmers who followed Daddy here were peaceful men. They were ahead of their time. When the Indians are put back on their reservations to stay, the farmers can come and live in peace. Herman is fighting for that day."

"Why is he so set on getting the Wingates to move?"

"He isn't," Jennie said instantly with a show of temper. "It's Sandy Spurlock who wants to buy them out."

"I heard Sandy was sparking Martha."

"He is, or at least he was. Martha doesn't care much for him. He's too much of a fighter. She doesn't like violence."

"Maybe Dack is right. People who don't like fighters shouldn't be out here now."

"Martha told me she is even afraid of you. Solly Ingram was telling her about the fight you had the other night with Sandy and the Orrs. According to Solly, you did pretty well for yourself."

"I handed out a few sore spots," Wade said. "You can tell Martha that I don't fight women that way."

Jennie giggled. "Why don't you tell her yourself?"

Wade felt his face flush. "Easy, Jennie. You're jumping off the wagon."

"I think I know where I'm landing, "Jennie said. "I'm all for you, Wade. They don't come any nicer than Martha." She glanced at the west where the sun had disappeared. "Let's go back. I'm afraid out here after dark."

Wade rode back into town with Jennie.

It was at breakfast two days later that Solly broke

some news to Wade that sent him into quick action.

"The Orrs closed their blacksmith shop and went to Junction City," Solly reported.

"How do you know where they went?" Wade asked.

"They left a sign on their door saying they were going to Junction City for supplies."

"Why did they both go?"

"You got me there," Solly said, scratching his head. "Must be an important load of stuff they're bringing in. Why don't you go to Junction City?"

"Think I will," Wade said. "Dad needs some lumber for the front of his store, Jennie says. Junction City is the closest place we can get it without sawing it ourselves, isn't it?"

"Reckon it is. But make the trip a fast one. I want you here for our services Sunday."

Wade grinned as he left the table. "I haven't missed church since I came here, have I?"

Jason Harper seemed very pleased when Wade told him he wanted to take his team and wagon to Junction City for lumber for the store. By the middle of the forenoon Wade was ready to go.

It was a long hard day's drive with a wagon from Paradise to Junction City. Wade would have cut the trip into two days if he hadn't been in such a hurry to get to Junction City and find out, if possible, what the Orrs were up to.

As it was, he got into town about midnight. He put his team up in a livery barn and crawled into the hay in the loft to get some sleep.

Wade had no trouble locating Bradley and Ardy Orr the next day. They were loafing around town as though they had nothing in the world to do. Their wagon was standing empty in the yard beside the livery barn. Wade's curiousity burned hotly, but he couldn't manage to corner either of the Orrs to talk to him.

Wade loaded the lumber he had come to buy. But he kept on eye on the Orrs' wagon. At sundown it was still standing empty and neglected. Evidently the cargo they had come for hadn't arrived in Junction City.

That raised Wade's suspicions and curiosity to fever pitch. He checked the wagon once more before going to bed. It was still empty.

Wade slept well. The Orrs weren't liable to leave in the night, especially when their wagon wasn't even loaded.

But Wade got a rude shock when he went down to the livery stable the next morning after breakfast. The

Orrs' wagon was gone. He cornered the stable owner and asked about it. The man shrugged.

"They left about midnight, I reckon. Said they didn't want to work their team so hard, so they would travel at night while it was cool."

"Were they loaded?" Wade asked.

"How do I know?" the man growled. "I don't pry into my customers' business. But I reckon they'd be fools to come this far and then go back empty."

Wade agreed with that logic. He got his team out of the barn as quickly as he could get them harnessed. Hitching up, he pulled out of town just as the sun was coming up.

It was deep twilight by the time he came to the crossing of the Solomon River. Trees lined the river banks, and Wade was tempted to halt for the night.

But thoughts of rest vanished with the explosion of a rifle. Wade heard the bullet snap past his head. Jerking the team to a halt, he rolled off the high seat, dropping down on the lumber inside the box.

That rifleman wasn't too far away, somewhere in those trees. It must have been the half-darkness that had made him miss his target.

Another bullet slapped into the wagon box inches

above Wade. The team lunged ahead for the reins had slackened when Wade dived off the seat. Wade didn't dare lift his head to see where the team was going, for the rifle was still singing a death chant.

Then the wagon slammed to an abrupt halt as it struck a tree. Wade was thrown against the front of the box, but his shoulder cushioned the shock. He was up and over the side of the box almost before the wagon came to a complete rest.

Ducking behind a big cottonwood, he waited for the rifleman to reveal himself. Wade was so mixed up now that even his sense of direction was gone. After a tense minute of absolute silence, he shifted slightly to get his gun in his hand.

That move brought the sharp report of the rifle again, and Wade dived to one side. The rifle was behind him and close. Wade was pinned to the ground.

VII

Dirt and pebbles showered into Wade's face as a second bullet missed its mark by only inches. Wade chose that instant to lunge to his feet and around a tree. Another bullet slapped bark in his face; the rifleman was using a repeater.

Wade exchanged a few shots with the rifleman; then he heard the crack of a dry limb and saw a shadow dodging away through the trees. He squeezed off another shot but knew he had missed.

Judging from what he had seen, Wade guessed the ambusher might be Spurlock.

Wade dodged through the trees after the man for a short distance, then stopped. He had escaped the ambush without serious injury. He'd be a fool now to charge blindly after the man, who would probably get a load or two in his rifle and wait for him, making the job he had already bungled easy for himself.

Wade turned back to his wagon. The most serious damage to the wagon was a broken tongue. Pieces of the tugs were still hooked to the singletrees where they had broken, and one singletree was snapped in two. It would take some time to fix up the mess. And the horses were missing.

Wade started along the river through the trees in the direction the horses had been going. Tired as they were from the hard day on the road, they couldn't have run very far.

He found them less than a quarter of a mile away, still hitched together with the neck yoke, the tugs of one horse trailing the pieces of the singletree. They submitted docilely to Wade's guidance, and he led them back to the wagon.

Wade examined the wagon and harness and decided it would take hours to repair the damage, even if he had had the necessary tools. He stripped the harness off the horses, leaving only the bridles. Then, taking his rifle from the wagon box, he straddled one horse and, leading the other, crossed the Solomon and headed west toward Paradise.

The delay had cost him a lot of time, and it was almost daylight when he rode into the silent town. He put the horses in Jason's barn just east of the store building and went down the quiet street toward Solly's.

The next morning, immediately after breakfast, he went outside and moved up the street. The blacksmith shop was open, and both Bradley and Ardy Orr were lounging in the doorway as Wade went past. Their wagon was standing west of the shop, empty. Whatever they had hauled from Junction City was already unloaded and installed in the shop.

Wade hurried on down to the store to explain to Jason what had happened. Anger clouded Jason's face when Wade explained how the wagon and harness had been broken during the ambush on the Solomon. The anger expressed itself in hot words when Wade said he had something to do that morning instead of riding back to the Solomon to fix the wagon and harness. Jason finally agreed to do it, leaving Jennie in charge of the store.

"What have you got to do that is so important?" Jennie asked Wade as he was about to leave the store.

"Find out why somebody tried to kill me last night, for one thing," he said. "I was trying to catch up with the Orrs and their wagon last night when I was ambushed. They seem to be pretty particular who sees what they haul in from Junction City. I aim to find out what they're hauling."

"If you were ambushed once—" Jennie began.

"I may be again," Wade finished. "But I have my own reasons for taking that chance."

Wade turned up the street toward Solly's again.

Ardy Orr was still loafing in the doorway of the blacksmith shop as Wade went past. He spat a stream of tobacco juice into the dust just inches short of Wade's feet, but Wade ignored him. He had no time for a fight with Ardy now.

Men were working on the new livery barn and corrals being built down by the river. It would be the only place of business on the river side of the street.

Wade got his horse and rode up on the bluff. Slowly he cut across the prairie north and west of town, looking for fresh wagon tracks. On the road that led out to Wingate's, he found them. He followed at a lope, for they were easy to see. They led close to the Wingate farm, and Wade reined into the yard. Wingate was in the field beyond the barn, but Martha came to the door when she heard him.

"See any wagon go by here early this morning?" he asked.

"Why, no," Martha said. "But I do remember hearing one before daylight. I thought it was one of our neighbors up the river getting a real early start for Junction City."

"Was the wagon going east?"

Martha moved closer to Wade's horse. "I don't remember. I guess I didn't pay much attention. Is something wrong?"

"A wagon went by here real early this morning, heading west. I was hoping somebody had seen it and could tell me who was driving."

"Only the Hebrons and Bellings live west of here," Martha said. "I can't imagine what they'd be doing going home at that hour."

"Neither can I," Wade said, and reined his horse around. "Tell your dad to keep a sharp watch."

"Is there more trouble?" Martha asked, worry in her voice.

"Maybe not," Wade said, almost wishing he hadn't said anything. "I was in Junction City a couple of days ago. Lots of talk about the Indians. But probably most of it is just rumors."

"We'll keep on the alert. Pa carries a rifle with him all the time. And I've got one in the house."

"Can you use it?"

She tried to smile, a feeble effort. "Put on some war paint and try to sneak up on me and see."

He grinned. "I'll take your word for it. I'd rather come calling as a friend. Any objections?"

Color rushed up in her cheeks. "Of course not. We'd love to have you come. And bring Jennie, too."

She ran back to the house, and Wade urged his horse back toward the wagon trail.

The wagon track followed the dim road that led on to the two farms farther up the river. But before it reached those farms, the track swung back toward the river and into the trees, threading its way through them past the two farms.

It must have been light when the wagon had gone past these farms, Wade decided, and the driver hadn't wanted to be seen. When he came even with the closer of the two farms, Wade reined over to the man working in the small field and asked him if he had seen the wagon.

The man shook his head, lifting his hat to run a hand through his sweat-matted hair. "I ain't seen no wagon.

There ain't nobody west of me, mister. No wagon would be going up there."

"How about Ft. Hays?" Wade asked.

"Well, now I reckon that could be. But most freight heading for Hays goes on the railroad. If they went from Paradise to Hays, though, I reckon they might come by here."

The man turned back to his plow, and Wade returned to the creek to pick up the trail again.

The trail left the trees eventually and went back up on the prairie where the going was easier. Wade knew he was gaining on the wagon. The tracks were fresher. In one swale, he paused to study the sign and noticed blades of grass still springing erect after being pushed down by the horses' hoofs.

He went ahead then with more caution. The land was furrowed with washes and dry gullies running into the river. Each time Wade came to the top of one of the ridges, he moved cautiously until he had scanned the ridges ahead.

Finally the tracks led down to the river and across it. Wade decided that the wagon might very well be heading for Ft. Hays. He crossed the river and again began the game of hurrying through the gullies and peeking cautiously over the ridges before riding quickly over into the next wash.

Then as he neared the top of a low ridge, he suddenly reined his horse back down the slope. On a high ridge less than half a mile away were two riders, Indians. Wade didn't need a map to tell him that he was deep in Indian territory now.

Those two Indians might be friendly. But most of the friendly Indians were loafing around the forts and settlements, begging their living. These two didn't look like the loafers Wade had seen. He certainly had no inclination to find out if they were.

He reined around, putting his horse to a lively canter, and headed back to Paradise.

VIII

The next day Wade decided to see if Dack was back.

Dack was in the back of the store, Jennie told Wade. He had arrived home the day before Wade got back from Junction City. In time to send Spurlock out after me, Wade thought.

Dack came into the store, and Wade turned on him.

"Just where did you go this time and what for?" he demanded.

Dack's fixed smile faded a little. "I hardly think I have to answer to you for all my actions," he said sharply. "But if it will satisfy you any, I was looking for good solid citizens that I could interest in our community."

"Any luck?"

Dack shrugged. "Not much. People aren't interested

in moving out onto the prairie this late in the summer. Some of those I talked to may come next spring, though. I did find a man to come and run the livery barn for us."

"So I just heard," Wade said. "A real gunslinger, Red Sloan."

"He'll make a good citizen of Paradise," Dack said easily. "He may be good with a gun. But out here, with the Indians going more on the warpath all the time, that's an asset, not a liability. I also got something else for our town: a piano."

"A piano," Wade echoed ."What for?"

"First and foremost," Dack said importantly, "for the dance we're staging to celebrate the opening of our new business, the livery stable."

"Where can we hold a dance in this town?" Jennie asked.

"In Sandy's saloon. We'll clear out everything but the bar, put the piano at the north end of the bar, and we'll have the whole room for dancing."

"When?" Jennie asked excitedly..

"This Saturday, if the piano and Red Sloan both get here in time."

Both arrived in time. The piano came in the next

day, and on the following day, Sloan showed up. Wade and Solly watched him ride into town and tie at the hotel hitchrack. Wade knew him from reputation rather than sight. Solly had seen him in Kansas City.

"Looks just like he did when I saw him," Solly said. "Red hair, freckled face and quick hands."

"He'd have to have those," Wade said, "to build the reputation he has."

"Be mighty careful around him."

"I expect to be," Wade said. "But I can't run from him. That would get me nowhere."

"Could keep you alive," Solly said.

Dack made sure that every family in the country that claimed Paradise as its town heard about the Saturday night dance. Dack found two men who could play the fiddle and another who could chord on the piano. It promised to be a big night.

When Wade went down to the store early Saturday evening to escort Jennie to the dance, mainly to keep Dack from doing it, he found Martha at the store, too.

"My folks aren't coming tonight," Martha explained, "so I came in to spend the night with Jennie. Pa doesn't want me to ride home after dark, alone or in company."

Wade nodded. "He's right. A troop of cavalry would hardly be safe out on the prairie these nights."

"The fellow that freighted in the piano said another family was wiped out on Smoky Hill between Harker and Hays," Jason said. "The soldiers couldn't find a trace of the redskins by the time they got there."

"What's it coming to?" Martha asked worriedly.

"The soldiers will have to whip the Indians," Jason said, "and run them back on reservations where they belong. Nobody's going to be safe until they do."

"The forts can't spare enough men to launch a campaign like that," Wade said. "At least that's what they tell me."

"So we just sit here like big fat pigeons," Jason said, shaking his head. "How can we coax people to come here until it's safe?"

"Let's go celebrate," Wade said. "This is no time to worry about what might not happen."

They started down the street, and Dack came out of the hotel, where he made his headquarters, in time to join them and parade into the saloon with Jennie on his arm.

It was a hot July night. Though there weren't too many people in and around Paradise, most of them were present, and the saloon couldn't accommodate them in comfort. Spirits were high, but Wade felt the tension in the dancers as they tried to make it appear they hadn't a care in the world.

Red Sloan came in, and a minute later Dack stopped the music and stood Sloan up on a stool beside the bar. Even then Sloan's head was only a few inches above Dack's.

"Here is our new citizen," Dack announced proudly, "Red Sloan. He'll operate our livery barn for us. We're glad to have him. Let's make him welcome."

As if to demonstrate his own appreciation of the new-comer, Dack led him over, introduced him to Jennie and offered her to Sloan for the next dance as though he owned her.

Anger burned inside Wade. It was bad enough to have Dack dancing with Jennie, but to have him toss her to a gunman like Sloan without even asking her permission was almost more than Wade could take.

He managed to get a dance with Jennie after Sloan left her.

"Do you know who that was you were dancing with?" Wade demanded none too gently as they fell in step with the music.

"Herman introduced him as Red Sloan," Jennie said coolly. "He seemed nice enough and he's very polite. I think he's a real gentleman."

"He's also a well known gunman. He was brought here to kill me."

Jennie jerked her head back and stared at Wade. "You don't mean that," she whispered.

Wade was astonished at the sudden change in her. The coolness, the superiority of a minute before was gone, and fear and genuine concern were in her voice.

"Don't worry about it," Wade said. "Nobody has killed me yet. I don't figure on letting Sloan be the first."

The waltz was only half over when Wade felt a tap on his shoulder. Turning, he saw Sloan grinning at him.

"Don't mind, do you?" Sloan said.

"Any reason why I should?" Wade asked. He studied Sloan's face before relasing Jennie. The grin was a friendly one. But it could be just a reflection of the anticipation inside the gunman.

Wade went back to the wall, where a dozen other men were lounging.

The dance would have ended without trouble in spite of Red Sloan's presence if it hadn't been for Spurlock.

Wade's attention was drawn to Spurlock and his dancing partner, Martha Wingate, not by any loud words but rather by the quality of Martha's voice. They were close to Wade, and he heard her words distinctly.

"I won't do it," she said in a low, cutting tone.

"You'll finish out this dance with me, anyway," Spurlock said, the anger in his voice poorly disguised.

Wade saw his arm tighten around Martha as she struggled to break free of his grip. Wade had no idea what the argument was about and he didn't care. He did care that Spurlock was forcing his attentions on Martha.

He moved quickly, threading his way between two dancing couples, and jerked Spurlock around.

"Let her go," Wade demanded.

"Keep your nose out!" Spurlock snapped, and threw a fist at Wade.

Wade ducked Spurlock's wild swing and lashed out with a blow of his own. Spurlock had no chance to duck, and the blow caught him squarely on the mouth. He staggered back; Martha barely managed to escape his fall.

He crashed against the bar and slid down on his haunches before he could catch himself. He struggled to his feet, dazed, and Wade slammed him down again.

Men stepped between them then, but the fight was over, anyway. Spurlock had no desire to go on.

Wade turned away. Martha brushed past him, and he turned toward her. "Do you think you can settle everything by fighting?" she said angrily as she went toward the door.

IX

Spurlock stepped out on the porch of the hotel as Wade passed. He had a cut on one cheek and his lips were swollen to testify to the force of Wade's blow the preceding night.

"You're taking your last walk down this street, Harper," Spurlock said, grim satisfaction in his voice.

"You figuring on seeing to that?" Wade asked, instantly on the alert.

"I don't have to kill you," Spurlock said. "Red Sloan took exception to the way you tried to play top dog last night at the dance. He's calling you."

"He hasn't told me anything about it."

"I'm telling you right now. Sloan will be waiting for you at the livery barn at nine o'clock this morning. He told me to tell you."

"And you'll be waiting here to plug me in the back if he misses, Is that it?"

Spurlock grinned. "Sloan won't miss. Don't forget. Nine o'clock."

Wade went on, leaving Spurlock leering after him. It was eight-thirty now. In half an hour Red Sloan was scheduled to do the job he had been brought here to do.

Solly came in shortly before nine. Excitement and anger were on his face.

"I just heard," he said. "Spurlock is spreading it over town that Sloan has challenged you. And he says you're going to show the white feather."

"Hadn't thought about it," Wade said. "But it's a senseless thing."

"It certainly is," Solly agreed. "Sloan has nothing against you; you've got no bone to pick with him. Spurlock has just hired him to do a job he's afraid to tackle himself. Get your horse and ride out of town, Wade. When you come back, maybe it will have blown over."

Wade grunted. "With Spurlock telling everyone that I've run out? If I don't face Sloan, I can't come back to this town. Spurlock has made sure of that."

"Sandy is a vicious man," Solly said. "A coward, too; afraid to do his own bad deeds. I wish Herman

Dack would take a hand. He could put a stop to this."

Wade was on the point of saying that it was all Dack's idea, but he checked himself. Nobody, not even Solly, would believe that. And Wade had a sudden idea that drove all others from his mind.

He glanced at the clock. Only five minutes to go. He walked to the door. He'd be facing east as he went toward the livery stable and corral. Sloan would have the sun at his back. But it would be high enough so it shouldn't bother Wade too much.

But Wade wasn't considering the sun. He took his gun out of its holster and laid it on the table. As he walked east, nobody on the north side of the street would be able to see that he wasn't wearing a gun. Only Sloan would see that.

"You're crazy," Solly exclaimed as he realized what Wade was doing. "Sloan can kill you, and nobody will know that you weren't armed. And if he doesn't kill you, they'll certainly say you were scared, going down there without a gun."

"I've got to do it this way," Wade said firmly. "Sloan doesn't want this fight any more than I do. I'm giving him a chance to get out of it."

"You're giving him a chance to carve an easy notch

on his gun."

"You want to see us shoot it out?"

"Of course not." Solly scowled. "But I don't want to see you murdered, either."

"You told me once, Solly, that you prided yourself in being able to see into a man's soul. Well, maybe some of that rubbed off on me. Last night I figured Red Sloan's the kind who doesn't really want to kill anybody. He's a killer more by chance than by choice. I'm going to give him a choice."

Solly shook his head doubtfully, but he held out his hand. "Good luck," he said.

Wade moved into the street, hitched up his belt as though bringing his gun within easy grip of his fingers, then started toward the barn that set back in the edge of the trees toward the river.

Red Sloan moved out in front of the barn. Wade expected Red to come forward to meet him, but he only stood there. Wade reached the end of the corral which had been built in the trees; more than a dozen big cottonwoods and elms were inside the corral. The barn was almost directly across from the blacksmith shop, and Wade saw both the Orrs standing in the doorway, watching eagerly.

Wade moved along the side of the corral, and Sloan crouched, waiting. Maybe he had misjudged him, Wade thought. Maybe he wanted this fight. If he did, the fact that Wade wasn't carrying a gun wouldn't stop him. For everyone knew why Wade had been called down there. Only a fool would answer such a call without a gun.

Wade passed the halfway mark in the corral, keeping his hands clear of his sides. Sloan watched him intently, his eyes squinted almost shut. Then suddenly they opened in astonishment and he came half out of his crouch.

"You mule-headed fool!" he breathed. "Where's your gun?"

"Back in the house," Wade said in a low voice. "If you're so set on killing me, I figure you can do it whether I have a gun or not."

"If you didn't come to fight, why did you come at all?"

Wade stopped. "To talk to you, Sloan. I've got an idea about you."

Sloan stood still for a moment, his hand still an inch from his gun, hanging there forgotten.

"All right," he said finally. "Come on into the

barn."

Wade was weak in the knees as he moved forward. He would probably never know just how close he had been to death as he came down along that corral fence.

"Now say your piece," Sloan said sharply as Wade stepped inside the barn. "Then either get your gun or get out of town."

"My piece will be short," Wade said. "I figure you to be a gunman but not a killer. You were hired to kill me, and I've got a good idea who's putting up the money. But you haven't got anything against me, and I haven't anything against you. Is it worth the money they're paying you to kill a man for no reason?"

Sloan stared at Wade, his face pulled down in a frown. "You're a queer one. You're right—I never killed a man before except with good reason. What's in it if I don't beef you?"

"Nothing," Wade said, "except one less notch on your gun and your conscience. Might be we'd even get to see things from the same side of the fence."

"What makes you think that?"

"I never yet saw a man who had any respect for another man who was afraid to do his own killing."

Sloan rubbed his chin. "You are a peculiar jaybird.

You're right again—I don't have any respect for the man who offered me the money for this job. But the money's good."

"Still planning to collect it?"

"Don't know," Sloan said, still frowning. "I never killed a man I liked. And I'm beginning to like you."

Wade nodded. "I guess that goes both ways. I like a man who comes out and says what he thinks."

"I'm not sure what I think now," Sloan said. "Better get out of here before I change my mind and decide to fatten my bankroll."

Wade grinned and went back outside.

X

Wade's respect for Sloan went up when it became obvious that the redhead wasn't going to tell the real reason there had been no fight at the barn.

"I don't favor any gunfighter," Solly said one morning at breakfast. "But I do admire Sloan. If it wasn't for his guns and his reputation, I'd like to have him for a friend."

"It's because of those guns and reputation that I'd like to have him for a friend," Wade said, grinning. "He makes a powerful argument just walking along beside you."

"I'm going to ride out to Wingate's today to see why they weren't at church last Sunday," Solly said. "Want to ride along?"

"Sure," Wade said quickly.

Solly grinned knowingly. "I thought so. Maybe Martha will be glad to see us."

Wade flushed. He had jumped at Solly's suggestion too quickly. "She won't be glad to see me," he said. "You forget I'm a violent man, and she doesn't like violent men."

Solly nodded. "You have a point there. But just how violent does she think you are?"

Wade shrugged. "You tell me."

"Afraid I can't. She'll probably never change her mind about disliking violent men. But she can change her mind in a hurry about just who is violent and who isn't. Don't ever underestimate a woman's ability to twist things around to suit her."

Wade moved toward the door. "I'll get my horse saddled," he said.

Wade had moved his horse to the new livery barn, using the excuse that Solly's horse was crowded in the little barn with Wade's horse there, too. Keeping his horse in the new barn gave Wade a better chance to check on the comings and goings of other riders and drivers in town. Sometime somebody would make the move that Wade was waiting for. When it happened, he wanted to know about it.

Red Sloan was alone in the barn, cleaning one of the stalls, when Wade walked in. He leaned on his fork and pushed his hat back from his mop of red hair.

"Looking for a horse or information?" he asked.

"Both," Wade said.

"I'm long on horses but short on information. Riding somewhere?"

"Going with Solly out to Wingate's," Wade said.

Sloan nodded wisely. "That figures. Say, I've got a question to ask you. You don't need to answer it if you don't want to."

Wade looked sharply at the redhead. "I'm listening."

"Has your sister got a steady beau?"

"Jennie?" Wade exclaimed. "Are you interested?"

"Any reason I shouldn't be?"

Wade shrugged. "I guess not. The field is wide open, I reckon."

"I had the impression Herman Dack had the inside track," Sloan said.

"A little competition scare you?" Wade asked.

Sloan grinned. "I don't spook very easy. I just didn't want to sit in against a stacked deck."

"I'm all for you," Wade said. "Now I'd like to ask

a question. Who was paying you to gun me down?"

Sloan eyed Wade steadily. "You know I'm a pretty plain talker. But I respect a man's confidence. I gave my word not to tell who hired me. So I'll keep my mouth shut."

Wade nodded. "I'll never ask you again. My horse handy?"

"Right in the corral. All grained for a big day."

"Don't expect a big day," Wade said, moving toward the back door of the barn. "Anybody else take his horse out today?"

"Dack got his about half an hour ago," Sloan said.

"Where was he going?" Wade asked, stopping in the doorway.

"He didn't say," Sloan said. "But he headed north out of town."

Wade had his horse saddled when Solly rode up. They climbed the bluff north of the buildings and angled northwest toward Vern Wingate's farm.

The late July sun was already hot on the prairie, and the wind, although out of the north, was doing little to cool the air.

"Going to be a scorcher," Solly observed. "We'll try to be back in town by noon."

Wade nodded without saying anything. He wondered why Solly had decided to ride out to Wingate's today. It wasn't just because the family had missed church last Sunday.

Then, less than halfway to the farm, Wade's attention was riveted on a puff of smoke rising on the wind to the northwest.

"Who would have a fire out there?" Wade demanded, apprehension gripping him.

"There's mischief afoot," Solly said. "Nobody would start a fire on a dry windy day like this without malicious intent."

Wade kicked his horse into a lope. The smoke was winging into the air now, and already he could locate the blaze. It was almost directly north of the Wingate farm. With a north wind, that fire could sweep directly down on the farm.

"Indians?" Wade yelled as he urged his horse faster.

Solly kept pace with him. "Maybe. We've got to warn the Wingates, anyway."

Wade had no other thought as he prodded his horse to the limit. The fire itself was plainly visible to the north when Wade and Solly charged into the Wingate yard. The Wingates had already seen the fire, and Vern had his team hitched to the plow.

Wade hit the ground before his horse was fully stopped. He threw the reins to Martha, who had run to meet them. "Tie my horse; then pump water. Soak every board in your buildings, especially on the north side."

"We can't stay here," Mrs. Wingate screamed, pulling at her husband's arm. "We'll be burned to death."

Vern jerked away. "I'm going to save my place," he yelled, and slapped the reins on his team.

Wade left the job of soaking the buildings to Solly and the women while he ran to take the handles of the plow.

"Drive fast," Wade urged. "Maybe we can beat it."

Four times Vern swung the team across the north side of the buildings. Wade held the plow so that it turned a thin layer of sod, grass down.

"That should do it," Wade yelled. "Put your team up and help pump water. I'm going to start a backfire."

Smoke was swirling down over the yard now, getting in Wade's throat and making his eyes water. But he had no time to think about his discomfort. If they didn't get a strip of prairie burned off north of the buildings, they would all go up in smoke.

The fire hadn't come as fast as Wade had at first feared it might. That was due to the green grass mixed with the dry, he decided. If they'd only had rain in the last couple of weeks! But that particular area had been without rain for several weeks now, and most of the grass was tinder dry.

Wade found a stick, wrapped a rag around it, soaked it in some kerosene that Martha got for him, then mounted his horse. Riding to the northeast about twenty yards beyond the strip of ground he and Vern had plowed, he stopped and touched a match to his torch. Then, putting his horse to a trot, he rode west, dragging the torch through the dry grass, leaving a line of fire in his wake.

When he had traveled the length of the plowed strip, he dropped the torch and wheeled his horse back into the yard. Tying the horse securely south of the barn, Wade joined the other, waiting with buckets of water and soaked rags and sacks along the edge of the plowed ground.

The backfire reached the plowed ground while the main fire was leaping high a couple of hundred yards to the north. Wade had no time to watch what the others were doing as he whipped out each spark that jumped the plowed barrier.

Then the backfire died out for lack of fuel, leaving a black strip twenty yards wide between the buildings and the fire bearing down on the farm.

"Solly, get the women on the other side of the house," Wade shouted above the roar the fire was making. "Vern and I will try to keep the buildings from catching fire."

The fire roared up to the burned-over strip, where the blaze sputtered and died of starvation. Flames ate along the grass at the sides of the burned-over strip and raced past the buildings. When the main blaze was past, Wade and Vern whipped out the little fires left behind by the head fire.

"Where will it go?" Martha asked as they put out the last spark and stood panting, exulting in their victory.

"When it hits the river it will die out," Wade predicted. "Nothing but prairie between here and the creek, and it won't jump the river, I'm sure."

Vern stood looking out at his cornfield. "The corn is ruined," he said dully. "A whole summer's work."

"We've still got our home," Mrs. Wingate said.

"What will we live on?"

Wade looked out at the field. The corn was still standing, but the heat from the fire had curled the leaves, completely scorching the stalks close to the edge of the field. Vern was right. The corn was ruined.

"Was it Indians who set that fire?" Martha asked, her voice little more than a whisper.

Wade shook his head. "It doesn't figure that way. If Indians had started that fire, they'd have aimed it at the town. This fire had no chance of hitting the town. And Indians would have followed in for the kill after the fire."

"Then who and why?" Vern demanded.

Wade shook his head. "I don't know. Solly, can you help them get straightened up here? I've got some riding to do."

"Watch yourself," Solly warned as Wade went toward the barn for his horse.

Wade rode east where the strip of burned prairie was narrowest. He found the place where the fire had started in a little gully about a mile north of the Wingate farm.

The fire hadn't started from a pinpoint such as might have happened if a careless man had tossed down a match. There were a dozen starting points all in a row along the gully bank.

The fire had been deliberately set in a wide enough line to insure a roaring blaze two hundred yards wide by the time it reached the farm buildings. If Wade and Solly hadn't been at the Wingate farm that morning, chances were that the fire would have accomplished its purpose.

Wade searched the ground along the gully but, other than horse tracks, he found nothing. The ground was too dry and hard to show where a human foot had stepped.

He got back to town before Solly rode in. He went directly to the saloon and found Spurlock loafing behind the bar. Red Sloan was leaning on the bar talking idly to Spurlock.

"He been here all morning?" Wade asked, jerking a thumb at Spurlock.

Sloan nodded. "Guess so. If he left town, he walked or rode somebody else's horse."

"What's eating you?" Spurlock demanded.

"Nothing that would interest you," Wade said, and went out into the street again.

If Spurlock had been in town all morning, that left the Orrs or Dack.

Wade found Dack's horse at the hitchrack in front of the store. Excitement rose in him as he saw the black ashes on the horse's feet. That horse had been in the burned area.

"Find something interesting?" Dack asked from the porch where he looked down on Wade.

Wade straightened, glaring at Dack. "Where did your horse get these black ashes?"

Dack shrugged, confidence oozing from him. "Out in the fire area. I rode over to see if I could help the Wingates after I saw the blaze. Too bad about that fire."

Wade's excitement died. For a moment he had thought he had Dack between a rock and a hard place. But Dack had had a perfect explanation, as usual.

"It sure is too bad, isn't it?" Wade said, still glaring at Dack.

Wade was positive Dack had started the fire. But he had no proof.

XI

July melted into August under the hot Kansas sun. Still Vern Wingate stayed on his farm. A rider came in from Abilene with more stories of Indian raids and atrocities. Paradise became as jittery as a skittish colt.

But it took some news relayed to Wade by Red Sloan to jolt him to his shoes. Sloan was sunk in depression when Wade came to the barn for his horse.

"Looks like you guessed wrong," Sloan said, "about Jennie being available."

Wade was on the alert instantly. "What makes you think so?"

"Jason gave me his word last night that Jennie and Dack are getting married. I suppose you'll stand up with Dack?"

The breath hissed through Wade's clenched teeth.

So that was how it was! He had waited too long for something to break.

"One of us won't be standing anywhere at that wedding," Wade said fiercely.

"Is it that bad between you two?" Sloan asked.

Wade nodded. "That bad. Never mind the horse. I've got some other business to take care of."

He wheeled up the street to the store. Dack might be there. But Dack could wait a few minutes longer. Right now he had to see Jason—to confirm the story Sloan had told him.

Jason was alone behind the counter when Wade went in. Wade wasted no time.

"I hear Jennie and Dack are getting married."

Jason nodded. "It will be a fine thing," he said, his face beaming. "Some day Herman will be Governor of the state, and Jennie will be first lady. You couldn't wish for anything more for her, could you?"

"She'll never marry Dack," Wade said.

"She will," Jason snapped, "this fall. You keep out of it, Wade. I know you don't like Herman, but that's no reason to ruin your sister's happiness."

"Happiness with Dack?" Wade exploded. "I told you what kind of a varmint he is. Do you expect her to be happy with a man like that?"

"She'll be a lot happier than she would be with that gunman, Sloan."

"Sloan is a man who fights in the open," Wade said. "He doesn't degrade the women he knows. I say he's twice the man Herman Dack is."

He strode past the counter toward the door that separated the store from the living quarters. Jennie was washing dishes when Wade walked in.

"Come outside, Jennie. I want to talk to you."

Jennie dried her hands and untied her apron. "My, but you're bossy this morning."

"I'm mad," Wade said.

He waited until Jennie had the apron off and laid over the back of a chair; then he led the way outside. The sun was well up, and the day promised to be a hot one.

"Now what are you mad at?" Jennie asked. "Me?"

"Maybe," Wade said. "Dad told me and he told Red Sloan, too, that you were going to marry Dack."

"Pa doesn't like Wilbur. He says he's a killer."

"Wilbur?" Wade echoed.

Jennie laughed. "That's Red's real name. I had quite a time prying it out of him. But Red sounds so undignified."

"Red's a square-shooter," Wade said. "He's handy with a gun, all right. But he's no killer. If he was, he'd have killed me that day at the corral when he had the chance."

"You like him and you don't like Herman. Why?"

"I know both men, Jennie. You aren't going to marry Dack, are you?"

Jennie's lips tightened into a narrow line. "Herman is a fine man, Wade. Some day he'll be an important man, too. Pa wants me to marry him."

"Dad's already married to him," Wade said bitterly. "That doesn't mean you have to be, too."

Anger flushed Jennie's cheeks. "If I want to marry Herman, that's my business."

Wade looked away, fighting his anger.

"Where is Dack now," he asked, his voice tight.

"He left for Junction City early this morning," Jennie said, relief in her voice. "He said he might even go to Kansas City."

Wade slammed a fist into his open palm. He'd have to wait a few days longer. But the minute Dack got back to Paradise, the waiting would be over. Probably Jennie would cut him out of her life and Jason might even do worse. But Herman Dack would never marry Jennie unless he killed Wade first!

The hot days dragged by for Wade. Dack didn't come back to Paradise. On the morning of the seventh of August, as Wade was passing the livery barn, he was waved inside by Red Sloan.

"What's eating you?" Wade asked.

"You want to keep posted on who leaves and comes, don't you?"

Wade's interest quickened. "I certainly do. Did Dack come in?"

Sloan shook his head. "The Orrs left this morning with their heavy wagon. Went east."

"Another trip to Junction City," Wade said. He rubbed his chin thoughtfully. "Last time they went I tried to follow them and find out what they were hauling. Got ambushed for my trouble. This time I'll just wait until they bring in their wagons. Then I'll surprise them."

Sloan shrugged. "I don't know what you're talking about. But it sounds like fun."

"The Orrs are hauling something from Junction City that they don't seem to want anyone to see. They brought in a load the last of June, just before you came. When I tried to trail them, I was ambushed. This time I'm going to see what they're hauling."

"Mind if I get my finger in the pie? This town is pretty dull for me. There might be some excitement when you pry into their wagon."

"I imagine there will be," Wade said. "I could use some help, if you want to buy in."

Wade didn't expect the Orrs back for at least two days, and it would more than likely be the tenth before they came. They wouldn't be crowded this time by Wade's presence in Junction City.

It was hard waiting. Each day Wade checked with Sloan and at the store. Dack still hadn't returned.

Then, about noon on the ninth of August, a man rode in from the southwest and racked his horse in front of the saloon. The men of the town began gathering at the saloon. A visitor was rare in Paradise, and one coming from the west or southwest could very well bring news of the Indian unrest.

Wade went to the saloon along with Solly. The man had quenched his thirst and was leaning against the bar, facing his growing audience. His clothes and the deep leathery tan on his face and neck marked him as a man of the plains.

"Where are you from?" Jason Harper asked as soon as he came in.

"My last stop was Ft. Larned," the man said.

"Where are you heading?" Spurlock asked.

"For Delphos," the man said, propping his elbows on the bar behind him. "I got a sister there. If you've got any sense, you'll be getting out of here."

"Indians on the warpath?" Jason asked.

The man nodded. "I figure they soon will be. I've been scouting for the army out of Ft. Larned. But I got my fill of it when they handed over all those guns to the redskins."

"Guns?" Jason exclaimed.

"You heard right. That was about four days ago. General Sully, in command at Ft. Larned, gave rifles to a party of those murdering Indians. They said they had to have them to kill game for their winter meat. General Sully believed them. He thinks this will make them more peaceful."

"You don't agree?" Solly asked.

"I ain't been scouting those sneaking whelps for ten years for nothing. They don't need more guns to kill buffalo. But they do to fight the whites. A lot of white men will die from those guns the Cheyennes got at Ft.

Larned. Mark my words. I made up my mind if the army was going to hand out guns and then wait to be shot, it could get along without this scout."

The scout turned back to the bar, his story finished.

"Are you going to stay with your sister until the Indian scare is over?" Solly asked, his face thoughtful.

"I'm going to get her out of there," the scout said. "There ain't no place this side of Junction City except Minneapolis that will be safe from those redskins now. And I ain't so sure Minneapolis will be safe."

Solly nodded and went out the door, Wade at his heels.

"What do you make of it, Solly?" Wade asked as they turned down the street toward home.

"I don't like it," Solly said. "That fellow is rather long winded. But I believe him. He's expecting trouble along these rivers. I've got to get word out to the Bellings and the Hebrons."

"You'll be sticking your neck into trouble if that scout is right," Wade said.

"Maybe," Solly admitted. "But somebody has to warn them."

Wade helped Solly make his preparations to ride out. When he left, Solly said he would spend the night with the Bellings and be back the next day, probably with the Belling and Hebron families in tow. The scout had had no proof that the Indians were on the warpath—he had just voiced his own opinion. And that wasn't enough to make the town run.

The scout had ridden on northeast toward Delphos and Paradise settled down to wait nervously.

Wade haunted the livery barn. Any time now it was possible that the Orrs might come in. If they made it tonight, it would mean that they had pushed their team hard. But there was no predicting what the Orrs might do.

Wade was at home, however, when Red Sloan came to the door, panting from his run across from the livery barn. Wade threw open the door at his knock.

"The Orrs back?" he asked quickly.

Sloan shook his head. "I don't think they'll make it tonight. It's Spurlock."

"What about him?" Wade demanded when Sloan paused to catch his breath.

"He took his horse out just now. Said he was going out to visit Martha, whether she wanted him to or not. I thought you'd want to know."

"Thanks," Wade said, grabbing his hat. "If he

pushes his way in, he'll have a showdown with Vern. And Vern will get killed."

"That's how I figure it," Sloan said. "I had to wait until Spurlock was out of sight before I came up here. I saddled your horse while I waited."

"Good," Wade said. "Maybe I can get out there before he does. He may not be so anxious to push his luck with me."

Sloan grinned. "I don't figure he will."

It was almost dark when Wade rode out of town.

The Wingate farm was quiet when he came in sight of it. There was no light in the window but Wade hadn't expected there would be. Wingate had been in town that afternoon and had been told of the warning the scout had brought. There would be no lights in any windows tonight.

Wade reined his horse off into a little swale and dismounted.

The surrounding prairie remained deathly quiet as the long hours dragged by. Wade mounted and rode slowly around the Wingate buildings. There was no sign of Spurlock.

Wade branded himself a fool. He had wasted half a night on the prairie, guarding a family that neither knew about nor wanted his concern. What about Spurlock? Why had he told Red Sloan that he was coming out to see Martha and then failed to show up?

As the answers began to form a pattern in his mind, Wade urged his horse to a lope toward town.

Once there, he reined in at the livery barn and dismounted.

Red Sloan, sleepy-eyed, answered Wade's banging on the door. "What's the idea?" Sloan asked. "Can't a man get any sleep?"

"Spurlock never showed up out at Wingate's," Wade said. "That must have been a trick to get me out of town. Have the Orrs pulled in?"

Sloan shook his head. "Nope. If they had, they'd have brought their team here, because they took the team they keep in my barn."

"Then why did Spurlock coax me out there," Wade said, rubbing his chin with a fist.

The sleep suddenly vanished from Sloan's eyes. "Hey, wait a minute. Seems like I remember hearing something an hour or two ago. I thought at the time if it was the Orrs, they'd be waking me up to put their team away. When they didn't I forgot it."

"You mean they might have come in?"

Sloan nodded. "I reckon they could have put their team in that little barn in the back of their blacksmith shop. They used to keep both their teams there before this barn was built."

"Let's look," Wade said, and led the way across the street.

They went along the side of the squat building to the barn in the rear. The door was half open, and Wade poked his head inside. It was pitch dark, and he moved in where he could check the two double stalls. A team of horses stood in one stall; the other stall was empty.

"Only one team," Wade said in a whisper.

"Right," Sloan agreed. Then suddenly he added excitedly, "Say, this team has been used hard. Dried sweat all over them."

Wade ran a hand over the hip of the nearest horse. There was a crust of dried lather stuck to the hair along the flank.

"They brought in their load, all right," Wade said. "Then they switched teams and went on. Where?"

"If I hadn't been such a deadhead I might have found out," Sloan said disgustedly.

"I'll find out," Wade said. "A wagon can't travel as fast as a saddle horse."

"You can't track a wagon till it's light," Sloan said. "Come on. I'll get you some breakfast while you wait."

Wade fretted away the time until the light of a new day softened the shadows in the street. Then he mounted his horse just as the door of the blacksmith shop across the street opened. As he rode out of town, Wade saw Bradley Orr standing in the doorway, glaring after him. Wade wondered if Ardy was behind his father— or if he was on the wagon Wade was following.

Wade had no trouble finding the track of the wagon, heading west just like the one that he had trailed over a month before. The iron tires had left clear marks in the wet grass.

Unlike the course taken before, however, this trail did not swing across the upland past Wingate's.

Wade rode rapidly, but still the time sped by. The dew on the grass dried in the sun and the tracks became harder to see. Wade had lost count of the hours when his eyes, scanning the horizon ahead for a sign of the wagon, saw instead a column of smoke. He reined in, every sense alert.

That smoke had no reason for being there. Maybe it was the Orrs' wagon. But he discarded that idea instantly. There was too much smoke to have been caused by a burning wagon, regardless of its cargo. It seemed to be just about where the Hebron homestead was located. A minute later a wisp of smoke appeared on the horizon to the right of the first column. That would be the Belling farm, Wade decided.

Now he knew. All thought of the wagon vanished, and he wheeled his horse, spurring him into a run. First he had to get the Wingates on the move; then he'd warn the town. That scout yesterday had known what he was talking about. The Indians apparently were making use of the rifles they had gotten at Ft. Larned.

His horse was in a lather when he came in sight of the Wingate homestead.

Wade reined to his left to reach Vern Wingate where he was mowing wild hay in a valley west of the house. It took only a few words of explanation to make Vern unhook the tugs and slap his team into a trot toward the house. He ran along behind, gripping the lines.

Wade rode on to rouse the women. When Vern came panting into the yard, Mrs. Wingate and Martha were already piling their most valuable things into the wagon.

"How much time do we have?" Martha asked as she ran past Wade with a small box.

"I wish I knew," Wade said, worriedly watching the southwestern hills. "It depends on how long they stay at those other farms to gloat."

Vern hooked the team to the wagon. "Come on," he yelled. "Let the rest of the stuff go."

His wife threw in an armful of things and climbed up on the seat of the wagon.

"I'll ride my horse," Martha said. "He's already saddled. I don't want the Indians to get him."

Vern Wingate slapped the lines, and the team, though tired, broke into a choppy gallop.

"Let's get out of here," Wade said. "No sense in stretching our luck."

"I've got a box of keepsakes under my bed," Martha said suddenly. "I've got to save that."

Wade shook his head and followed Martha inside.

Martha was on her knees reaching under the bed for her box when he heard a sound that sent an icy chill down his back: the frenzied whoop of murder-bound Indians as they located another homestead to plunder.

XII

Martha jerked to her feet, the precious box under her arm. "What is that?" Her voice was little more than a whisper.

"Just what you think it is," Wade said.

He dashed into the main room and looked out the west window. They were coming over the hill a quarter of a mile away, eight of them. Probably just a few raiders branching out from the main war party.

Wade wheeled back and shot a glance through the south window. Vern Wingate and his wife were already over the first hill to the southeast. Unless they happened to top a hill where the Indians might see them, they should make it safely to Paradise.

But Wade's immediate task was to save Martha and himself.

"What will we do?" Martha asked frantically.

"Any place we can hide? We can't fight off that many."

"There's our root cellar. Pa built it last fall."

"Where?"

"East of the house."

Wade considered the situation quickly. If the Indians saw the saddled horses, they'd know someone was there. But as yet they hadn't seen the horses, for the house stood between the horses and the Indians. And the cellar was on the opposite side of the house from the raiders, too. There was a chance, although it was a slim one.

Running to the window in the east bedroom, Wade motioned to Martha. "Out here. You get in the cellar. I'll be along."

Martha slid through the window like an eel, and Wade followed. Then Martha caught his arm.

"Get in the cellar now while there is time."

"Got to turn the horses loose," Wade said. "If they see them, they'll keep looking till they find us."

Wade ran to the hitchrack and flipped the reins loose. Then, after giving each horse a slap, he watched them as they headed straight east toward a draw.

Wade ran toward the cellar where Martha was standing on the steps carved in the dirt, holding up the door. On the other side of the house, Wade could hear the pounding hoofbeats of the raiders' ponies and an occasional whoop as an over-eager brave gave voice to his anticipation.

Wade hurried down the steps of the cellar and let the door come down over the opening, leaving everything in pitch blackness.

"There's a bench over there," Martha whispered. "We can sit on it."

Martha reached out and found Wade's hand, then led him across the small cave. On the opposite end from the door was a bench about two feet wide. It was simply a ledge of dirt about two feet high that had been left for a shelf. Martha had to clear away some jars of vegetables that she and her mother had already stored for next winter's use.

"Think they'll find us?" Martha whispered as they sat down on the damp earth.

"Maybe not," Wade said, hoping his voice carried more conviction than he felt.

Above them, he heard noise, grunts and shouts as the raiders ransacked the house. Wade felt a shiver run through Martha, and he put a comforting arm around her.

"They'll burn everything," she whispered.

"I reckon so," Wade said. "But they won't find us."

Then Wade's assurance was shattered as the door of the cellar was jerked open. Martha gave a tiny gasp and was silent. Wade's fingers tightened on the gun in his lap.

The light from the doorway didn't reach back to the bench where Wade and Martha sat. The warrior would have to come down the steps before he could see them. He'd never go back up, Wade vowed.

Wade expected Martha to scream or do some foolish thing. But she sat perfectly motionless, and when he glanced her way, he saw that she was holding a pint jar in her hand, ready to throw it.

He watched the Indian start down the steps. In another second or two the red man would see them. Then Wade would kill him. But he stopped halfway down the steps. A guttural voice barked at him from above.

Wade didn't understand the Indian words, but he guessed from the tone of voice that it was a command. The brave on the cellar steps hesitated a moment, then grunted and retreated to the top of the steps.

"What happened?" Martha whispered after the Indian had vanished.

"They must be in a hurry," Wade said softly, trying to analyze the raiders' actions. "This is only a small chunk of the main party. Maybe they have to catch up with the others. Likely they hope to strike across country and get away before the soldiers can catch them."

"There are soldiers at Ft. Harker only about twenty-five miles away," Martha said.

"They know that. Maybe that's why they're in such a hurry."

They listened in silence to the crackle of flames as the wooden part of the house burned. Wade heard horses running, but still he waited.

"Stay here," he said finally. "I'm going to take a look."

Cautiously he moved to the bottom of the steps. The Indians had left the cellar door open. Wade could see the smoke from the fire. But there was nothing else in sight but the sky.

Slowly he went up the steps until he could see out. For a long minute he scanned the yard. Then he moved up to the top of the steps. Off to the northwest he saw them, riding away as fast as they had come.

"They're gone, Martha," he called.

Martha came up the steps. Only when she stood beside Wade and realized that the warriors were really gone did her composure break and a sob shake her. Wade put an arm around her.

"There's nothing to cry about now," he said. "They're gone."

She clung to him like a drowning man clinging to a raft. Finally she lifted her head and managed a faint smile. "I was too scared to cry before."

"So was I," Wade said, "if that's any help."

She looked up at him, and he bent his head and kissed her.

For a moment after he released her, she seemed too shocked to move. Then she backed away from him a step, the color rushing up in her neck and cheeks.

"Why?" she whispered.

"I guess you know," he said.

The color mounted higher in her face, and she turned to look toward town. "Looks like we'll have to walk," she said.

"Walking isn't crowded," he said. He held out his hand. Shyly, like a bashful child, she took it. He struck off down the road toward town, Martha beside him.

On top of the second knoll, Wade saw their horses to the northeast. They hadn't run far and were now contentedly grazing. Martha's horse was easy to catch, being a pet; and once he was caught, Wade's horse gave up the idea of keeping out of reach.

The town was unharmed.

Vern Wingate wasn't aware that the Indians had struck his farm until Wade told him. He shook his head at the news, but there was no real sorrow in his voice.

"I'm just glad none of us were caught by those savages," he said, his eyes on Martha.

Wade left Martha to explain to her parents what a close shave they had had. He turned to Red Sloan, who seemed to be uneasy about something.

"Solly hasn't come back," Sloan said. "He should have been back long before this."

A chill ran through Wade. "I saw Belling's and Hebron's farms burning this morning. I'm going out to take a look."

"I'm going, too," Sloan said. "I'm tired of sitting around waiting for something to happen."

Wade understood. Red Sloan was not a man to wait for excitement. He was the kind who made it.

"I can't figure why the Indians came so close to town and didn't make a pass at it," Wade said as he waited for Sloan to saddle his horse.

"Maybe I can," Sloan said. "I've been thinking about that half-breed, Ardy Orr, and the sneaky way he moves around. He lives in this town, you know. Maybe—"

Sloan left his thought unfinished, but Wade could complete it easily enough. The same thought had been nagging at the back of his mind for a long time. Maybe the Indians wouldn't destroy a town that was the home of an ally and blood brother.

Martha and Jennie were waiting outside the livery barn when Sloan brought his horse out to the hitchrack where Wade's horse was tied.

"Be careful, Wade," Jennie said. "The Indians might come back."

"Maybe," Wade said. But he wasn't looking at his sister. The concern in Martha's face was all that mattered to him now. "If they should come back, they're not likely to cover the same ground they did on the way north."

"There's some talk of leaving Paradise and going to Minneapolis," Jennie said.

"Might not be a bad idea," Wade said, swinging into the saddle. "Jennie, look out for Martha, will you?"

Jennie laughed as color flooded Martha's face again. "I'll do that, Wade. But who's going to look after me?"

"I'd do that if I was here," Red Sloan said quickly. "Martha, you keep an eye on Jennie till I get back. Then I'll take over."

It was Jennie's turn to flush. "Oh, go on with you," she said. "We'll be safe enough. We'll stay with the others. You two be careful."

Martha lifted her hand as Wade swung his horse away from the hitchrack, and Wade returned her wave.

"Looks like you've got it bad," Sloan said as they galloped out of town.

Wade grinned. "I've had it for a while, I guess," he admitted. "It's just beginning to show."

"Wish I could be as lucky with Jennie," Sloan said.

"Maybe you will be," Wade said, "if we can get rid of Dack."

A short distance beyond the point where Wade had first seen the smoke that morning, Wade and Sloan separated. Sloan went on toward the Belling farm; Wade headed northwest toward the Hebron farm.

Wade came to the farm without seeing any sign of

Solly. The feeling had been growing in Wade that he'd never again see Solly Ingram alive. The farm was completely destroyed, the buildings burned except for the sod walls. The cornfield had been trampled where fire wouldn't burn the green stalks.

Gingerly Wade poked around in the ashes of the house and barn. But he found no bodies. Evidently the Hebron family had been warned in time to escape.

Half an hour later, when Wade met Sloan midway between the Hebron and the Belling farms, Red had bad news. The Belling family hadn't escaped. Sloan's face was pale, the freckles standing out boldly over his nose.

"Everything was burned, of course," Sloan reported. "I found Belling himself and his two little boys in the yard. They had a hundred arrows in them, and were scalped and torn up until their own folks would hardly have known them."

"What about Mrs. Belling and the Belling girl? She was about twelve, wasn't she?"

Sloan nodded. "They were farther out on the prairie. I figure that Belling and the boys were killed right at first. The women weren't so lucky. Before they were killed and scalped, those red devils did everything that a savage can do to a woman. I tell you, Wade, I'm going to kill some of those devils if it's the last thing I ever do."

Wade felt sick as he turned to the east with Sloan.

Suddenly Sloan reined up, pointing to his left. "What's that over on that knoll?"

Wade looked and quickly reined his horse that way. He knew before he was halfway there that they had found Solly Ingram. He had no arrows in him. He had been shot and scalped. Everything, from his horse to his watch, had been taken.

"Didn't you say the Bellings were killed with arrows?" Wade asked.

Sloan shook his head. "They had a hundred arrows in them. But they had been shot first. I figure the red devils wanted to be sure there was no resistance, so they shot Belling and the boys, then took the women." He looked down at Solly. "They're going to pay for this, too. I'll get some of them!"

Wade nodded grimly. "Count me in on that."

XIII

Wade would have stopped and buried Solly Ingram, but Red Sloan reminded him of the danger that threatened Paradise, and Wade agreed that they had to see to the safety of the living before burying the dead.

"Tomorrow when everybody is safely in Minneapolis, we'll come back and give a decent burial to Solly and the Bellings," Wade said.

The town was bustling like a mother hen in a spring shower when Wade and Sloan rode in. They moved up the street, Wade taking in the activity with quick eyes. He spotted Ardy Orr leaning against the door of the blacksmith shop. Only Ardy and Bradley Orr seemed unaffected by the excitement.

"Ardy's back," Wade said softly.

"So I see," Sloan said. "I've got a hunch he knows

lot more about all this than he's telling. I'm going
o have a talk with him."

They put their horses in the barn, and Wade headed
or the store. He wanted to hurry the departure of his
family and the Wingates. As he passed the hotel, he
saw Sandy Spurlock inside, pacing the floor nervously.
Herman Dack was talking to him.

He found Jason behind the counter of his store,
handing out supplies with a free hand. Money seemed
o be a forgotten item.

"They're stocking up on grub to live on while they're
n Minneapolis," Jason explained. "We're all going
up there until the soldiers put a stop to these raids."

Wade nodded. "A good idea. Need any help?"

"You can help your mother and Jennie," Jason said.
"They're packing. They think they have to take prac-
ically everything. You know women."

Wade nodded and went on into the living quarters.
His mother and Jennie and Martha and her mother
were all helping pack. Almost everything movable was
being put in boxes or piled in the middle of the floor
ready to be loaded in the wagon.

"The wagon ready?" Wade asked.

"We're not going until tomorrow morning," Jennie

said. "Herman called a meeting of everybody in town just as soon as he got back. Some of the families here can't be ready to go until tomorrow. We can't leave them. Anyway, we couldn't get to Minneapolis now until after night. Herman thought it best that we all stick together and go first thing tomorrow."

"He's right," Wade said, finding it hard to admit Dack could be right in anything.

"What did you find out at Belling's and Hebron's?" Martha asked.

Wade sighed. "Bellings all dead. The Hebron family were gone. I think they must have gone straight to Minneapolis. Solly got part way back to town before they caught him."

Wade helped with the packing, trying to shut from his mind what he had seen west of town earlier today.

The sun was a little more than an hour from the western horizon when Red Sloan arrived at the store. He came to the partition door into the living quarters and motioned for Wade. Wade didn't hesitate, for he read the urgency in Sloan's expression.

"Something wrong?" Wade asked.

Red motioned toward the outside door, and Wade followed him into the street.

"Ardy tell you something?" Wade pressed.

"Yeah," Sloan said; "something I wasn't expecting. I wanted to find out about the wagonload of freight they brought from Junction City and then carted off to the prairie. So I coaxed him into a corner with a bottle I bought at Sandy's saloon. He's a pig for firewater, you know."

"What did he tell you?" Wade asked impatiently.

"Nothing about the freight," Sloan said. "But I got him drunk enough to talk, all right. He said he is going to kill you today."

Wade shot a glance down the street toward the blacksmith shop. "Did he give any reason for that sudden decision?"

"It's not so sudden," Sloan said. "And he gave me a good reason, one worth a thousand dollars."

"A thousand?" Wade exclaimed. "Somebody put a price on my head?"

Sloan nodded. "Ardy said Dack offered him that to kill you after I flubbed the job and he couldn't find another gunman to do it."

Wade's eyes squinted. "So Dack was the one who hired you to kill me?"

Sloan shrugged. "Dack himself never offered me a

penny. But I had a hunch he was behind it. This new deal, though, is strictly between Ardy and Herman Dack."

"I wish I could prove that," Wade said, thinking of Jennie and Jason. Proof that Dack had hired Ardy Orr to kill him should be enough to open their eyes.

"That's the nice part of the whole thing," Sloan said. "You can. At least, Ardy said he got something from Dack just this morning to seal the bargain. And he wasn't so drunk that he didn't know what he was talking about."

"What did he get?"

"He said he got that diamond ring that Dack has been flashing around."

"That must be worth four or five hundred dollars," Wade exclaimed. "Dack must really want me out of the way."

"And he doesn't want his own hands dirtied with the job. Wouldn't look good for a future politician."

"If I can prove that Ardy's got that ring, I'll have what I want," Wade said. "Where is Ardy now?"

"He was in one corner of the blacksmith shop when I left him," Sloan said. "I coaxed him over there to soften him up with that bottle. Bradley would have run

me out with a sledge hammer if he'd seen me feeding
him that whiskey."

"Suppose he's still there?"

"Maybe," Sloan said. "He didn't have the ring with
him when I was talking to him, and he wouldn't tell me
where it is."

"If I can get him alone, I'll find out where it is."

"He's part Indian," Sloan said. "He may be pretty
tight-lipped if he takes a notion to be."

"I can be mighty persuasive, too," Wade said grimly. "I'm guessing that Ardy was out west somewhere
last night and early this morning. He probably wasn't
on the raid that killed the Bellings, but I figure he had
a finger in the pie some way. Do you think I'll go easy
on him?"

Sloan's face darkened. "I could cut the heart out of
any man I thought had a hand in that."

"Stay out of this now," Wade said. "This is my party."

Wade started down the street toward the blacksmith
shop.

The door into the shop was a large one, yet Bradley
somehow managed to block it very effectively when
Wade reached it.

"Got some business here?" Bradley Orr asked.

Wade nodded. "I want to see Ardy."

"He's not looking for company," Bradley said.

"Does he always see just what he's looking for?" Wade took a quick side-step that propelled him past Bradley into the shop.

He couldn't see much inside the shop, for the windows were small, allowing only a minimum of light to creep in. Wade made a quick survey of the interior of the shop, moving toward each corner to make sure Ardy wasn't slumped there, a victim of the bottle Sloan had given him.

But Ardy was nowhere in sight.

"If you don't have any business in here, get out," the blacksmith snapped, dogging Wade's steps angrily.

"My business is with Ardy. Where is he?"

"Out," Bradley said. "I don't keep tabs on Ardy."

"You're keeping mighty close tabs on him right now, I'll wager," Wade said sharply, glaring at Bradley.

"Sloan got him drunk," Bradley said angrily. "He'll say anything when he's drunk."

"Meaning he might tell too much of the truth?"

"When he gets drunk, he doesn't know the truth from a lie."

Wade nodded and kept on looking. Bradley Orr wasn't a good liar. He was afraid to let anybody talk to Ardy while his tongue was loose.

Wade took a look into the living quarters and also into the little stable in the back of the shop, but he didn't see Ardy, and Bradley was getting more belligerent by the minute. If Wade stayed around any longer he was going to have a fight on his hands. And right now he just wanted to see Ardy; not fight with Bradley.

Wade went out of the blacksmith shop. Standing on the hard ground in front of the shop, he looked down the street, trying to decide where Ardy was most likely to be.

He checked every room in the hotel that was unlocked. Spurlock followed him around angrily but didn't try to stop him. Wade realized it was hopeless. If Spurlock and Bradley Orr had decided to hide Ardy in the hotel, it would have been a simple matter to put him in a room and lock it.

Wade went back to the street.

At the store, he found the packing practically done and Jennie fidgeting around, looking to see if there was anything else that she felt she must take. He called her into the yard behind the store.

"Red told me a while ago that Ardy Orr is out to kill me," Wade said bluntly.

Jennie's face blanched. "Be careful, Wade. Ardy is dangerous."

Wade nodded. "Especially when he has been offered a thousand dollars for the job."

"Who would pay him to kill you?" Jennie demanded indignantly.

"Ardy says it's Herman Dack."

Wade watched Jennie closely. The shock that his words gave her seemed to hold her speechless for a moment. Then anger poured up into her face and Wade knew he had lost his gamble.

"You hate Herman," Jennie said hotly, "but that's no reason for making an accusation like that."

"Think what you like," Wade said grimly. "I know it's so. Is Dack wearing his ring?"

"I suppose so. There has been too much excitement today to notice."

"Ardy says Dack gave him the ring this morning to seal the bargain."

"You know that's a lie!" Jennie said angrily. "Herman would never make such a bargain. Besides, he'd never part with that ring."

"He might—to get me out of his way. If Dack doesn't have the ring now, will you believe me?"

Jennie pinched her lips together. "He might have lost it."

"If I get the ring from Ardy Orr, will that convince you?"

She nodded, defeat in her eyes. Then the anger surged back. "But Ardy won't have the ring. Herman would never do what you say he has!"

Wade went to the counter where his father stood. Most of the shelves behind him were bare now. And there were very few people left in the store.

"Where's Dack?" Wade asked.

"I don't know," Jason said wearily. "I've been wishing for him for the last two hours. I've been swamped with work here."

Wade nodded. "You didn't expect him to help when there was real work to do, did you?"

He turned through the door. The hotel and saloon were about the only other places where he might be. Wade was positive of only one thing now—he had to find Dack and bring the issue between them to a head before Ardy Orr sobered up and began sneaking around, looking for a chance to slip a knife or a bullet into Wade's back.

Just outside the store, Wade bumped into Red Sloan, coming from the west end of the street.

"Find Ardy?" Wade asked.

Sloan shook his head. "But I found something else. I was looking for Ardy in the stable behind the blacksmith shop. You know that extra wagon the Orrs have there?"

Wade nodded.

"Well, I thought Ardy might be hiding in the bed of that wagon. He wasn't. But there's something else in there."

"What?" Wade demanded.

"I didn't get a chance to find out. I must have made some noise. Bradley came charging through the door from the blacksmith shop. I was lucky that he didn't see me. He had murder in his eyes."

"We'd better take a look in that wagon," Wade said, and started to move around Sloan.

Sloan caught his arm. "Let's wait till dark. That's only a little while now."

XIV

"It's dark enough," Red Sloan whispered in Wade's ear. "Let's take a look in that wagon."

"This isn't your fight," Wade said, hunching his shoulders away from the front of the livery barn where he had been waiting.

"I bought my chips quite a while ago. You're not throwing me out of the game now."

Wade nodded. "All right. Let's go."

They angled across the street and started along it toward Solly's place, then suddenly stepped into the shadows between two dark buildings. At the back of the buildings, they turned toward the blacksmith shop.

"It's not very dark yet," Wade said softly, looking ahead into the deepening dusk.

"We've got to have enough light to see what's in

that wagon without striking a match. That partition between the stable and the shop isn't much good. A light might show through."

Wade understood the reasoning and nodded silently.

The shed that bumped up against the blacksmith shop was quiet when Wade and Sloan reached it. Silently Sloan pushed open the door, and they moved inside.

Sloan led the way to the wagon standing against the north wall. Two stalls were on the south side, but only one team was there. Evidently Ardy hadn't brought back the team and wagon he had taken west the last time.

"Here," Sloan whispered as he climbed up on a wheel.

Wade stepped up on the tongue of the wagon and reached in. It was dark inside the wagon, but his fingers found a long, heavy box. Sloan climbed into the wagon and as quietly as possible pried the lid off the box.

"Half a dozen boxes like this in here," Sloan whispered.

Wade's fingers ran over the long barrel of a rifle inside the box. And suddenly he had the answer. The Orrs were smuggling rifles and probably ammunition to the Indians. They had good reason for not wanting anyone to see what they had in their wagon when they came from Junction City.

"Wonder why they left some here," Wade whispered.

"Probably trying to get a higher price out of Black Kettle," Sloan said. "The Orrs are greedy. They'll get all they can out of these guns."

"With the rifles the Cheyennes got at Ft. Larned and the ones the Orrs have been slipping to them all summer, they're ready for a war."

"They've started it, if you ask me," Sloan said bitterly. "Let's get out of here before we get into one of our own."

Halfway out of the wagon box, Sloan suddenly stopped and leaned back inside. He picked up a box about a foot square and held it up so the faint light from the open door struck it.

"Ammunition?" Wade asked softly.

Sloan grunted. "This isn't bullets. Take it and let's see what it is."

Wade took the box while Sloan climbed out of the wagon. Quickly Wade opened the box and ran his fingers through the contents. It was mostly coins, gold ones, he guessed. And there were rings and breastpins and watches.

"So that's how the Orrs get paid for their rifles," Sloan whispered.

Wade nodded, a burning anger tightened his throat. "The Indians pay the Orrs with the loot they get from raiding the homesteads."

"This must be what Ardy got for the last load."

Wade's finger suddenly touched a large watch, and he brought it up into the faint light.

"Solly's," he whispered, recognizing the heavy timepiece. "The Indians couldn't have had this in time to trade it for the guns. Ardy killed Solly himself."

"I'll personally cut his heart out," Sloan breathed.

"Not unless you get to him before I do!"

Wade's concentration on the watch in his hand was suddenly shattered by a sound behind him. Wheeling, he saw light shoot across the shed from the partition door leading into the shop. He dropped the watch, his hand slapping his gun. Sloan was making a similar move.

Then a heavy weight crashed against Wade, slamming him into the wagon and tearing his hand away from his gun. Dimly he realized that Sloan had been hit from behind, too. So there had to be at least three men attacking them in the stable.

Using the wagon box as a lever, Wade threw himself backward, driving his assailant into the partition wall.

For an instant the man's grip was broken and Wade twisted free. Then the other man lunged for him, and they rolled in the litter on the stable floor. The other man was strong, and Wade realized he must be either Ardy or Bradley Orr.

Suddenly the comparative quiet of the barn was shattered by the ringing report of a .45.

"Break loose, Wade," Sloan yelled. "Use your gun."

The sound of the shot had apparently startled Wade's opponent. Wade, straining to get free, suddenly broke the man's grip and rolled away.

He rose to a crouch, his gun in his hand. The darkness in the stable was almost like a mantle now. Wade couldn't even see the man he had been fighting with.

Then the darkness was split with streaks of fire as guns roared and the din threatened to blow out the walls of the stable. Wade joined in, making sure Sloan was to his right. That meant there were only enemies in front of him.

For an instant Wade saw the outline of a huge man

silhouetted against the dim light of the open outside door. Spurlock, he decided. Or it might have been Dack.

There were at least three guns belching fire at Wade and Sloan; maybe four. Wade moved with every shot he made. Even with all his moves, he knew the chances were that a bullet would tag him if this barrage kept up.

A man grunted heavily close to the door, and a minute later there was another wild cry. Then a figure darted through the doorway into the darkness outside.

Wade stopped firing, for suddenly there were no flashes to fire at. A moment later the partition door squeaked and Wade wheeled in time to see a man dodging away into the blacksmith shop.

For a long minute Wade didn't move, and the silence grew. Finally Sloan's whisper broke the quiet.

"You all in one piece, Wade?"

"Sure. How about you?"

"Same. I guess they're gone."

Wade moved cautiously. No bullet sought him, and he stood up.

"What made them give up?" Wade asked.

"If I knew," Sloan said, "I'd be wiser than I am

now. Come on. Let's take a look."

Cautiously Wade moved away from the wall and joined Sloan. Sloan lit a match, holding it far to his left. Carrying the match, he moved toward a bulky object close to the outside door that hadn't been there when they had come in.

Sloan held the match close, and when he straightened, Wade could see the satisfaction on his face.

"Bradley Orr," Sloan said. "That's one of the murdering snakes. He was just as much to blame for the slaughter out there on those homesteads as the Indians themselves."

"There were more in here than just the Orrs," Wade said.

"I know," Sloan said. "Let's take a look outside."

Wade followed Sloan cautiously into the alley.

"Ardy is half Cheyenne, you know," Sloan said. "In fact, he's a lot more Indian that he is white man. The only reason he lived with the whites was Bradley."

Wade nodded. "Now Bradley is dead."

"So he has no tie with white men any more," Sloan said.

"You don't think he ran out just now because he was afraid?"

"No," Sloan said. "I've been around Indians quite a bit in my time. Ardy thinks and acts like an Indian. The odds were against him getting us there in that dark barn. But we killed Bradley. He'll never rest till he either kills both of us or is killed himself."

"I reckon that goes both ways," Wade said grimly. "Solly was one of the best friends I ever had."

"Let's see if Ardy's left town," Sloan said. "Watch every dark corner."

Wade didn't need the warning. While Sloan moved slowly down the street toward Solly's place, Wade went up by the store. The street was swarming with men and some women, excited and frightened by the shooting. Wade explained to Jason about the smuggling and the death of Bradley Orr, and let him relay the information on to the people, most of them farmers waiting for morning and the general exodus to Minneapolis.

Wade went into the saloon and hotel. Spurlock was gone. He looked for Dack but couldn't find him, either. He asked Jennie about him. She said she hadn't seen him since supper time.

Wade met Red Sloan back at the livery stable. Sloan reported no sign of any of the men. They checked the barn. Spurlock's horse and saddle were missing.

"He must have figured we had the goods on him," Sloan said. "Well, good riddance."

"But what about Ardy? He didn't take a horse from his barn. No other horse is gone from here, is there?"

Sloan shook his head. "He might have taken one of your dad's horses. Or he might have left the way he came."

"How was that?"

Sloan shrugged. "I don't know. He took a team and wagon out of here. He didn't bring either one back. Still he got here. I figure he rode a horse and left him in the trees along the creek."

"Why?" Then suddenly Wade understood. "Unless it was a horse everybody in town would recognize."

Sloan nodded. "Solly's horse was missing, you know. Whoever killed him evidently stole his horse."

"I can't find Dack, either. How do you figure that?"

"I don't. There's no way we can tie him into that fracas tonight."

"I think there is," Wade said. "I've been thinking about him. You know, every time the Orrs went to Junction City for a load of guns, Dack left here a few days earlier. My guess is he bought the guns and had the Orrs deliver them for a tidy profit for all concerned.

Dack says he's going to be a big man in Kansas some day. It's going to take money to build himself up. That would be one way of getting the money."

"A dirty treacherous way," Sloan said.

"Dack is a dirty treacherous man," Wade said. "If I could only prove it to Dad and Jennie!"

"Find Ardy Orr and get that ring and you'll have it. You said Jennie would believe you then."

"Finding Ardy may be quite a job. If what you say about him is right, he'll head for the Cheyennes."

"It may take him several days to find them," Sloan said. "Everybody is leaving town, anyway. I don't take to the idea of holing up in Minneapolis while somebody else gets out and chases the Indians away from me."

Wade nodded. "You'd like to go with me on Ardy's trail?"

Sloan grinned. "Now you're talking. We'll find that sneaking half-breed and we'll get that ring. That will prove to Jennie what kind of a snake Dack really is."

"I almost forgot you had a personal interest in showing Dack up."

"I've got an interest, all right," Sloan admitted. "But by the time I can prove my point, Jennie will probably be Mrs. Herman Dack. And the day after I find that out, she'll be a widow."

"Which won't help your cause any."

"Sometimes a man's only reward is his personal satisfaction. I could get a lot of satisfaction out of keeping Dack from having Jennie."

XV

Paradise spent a quiet night after the excitement of the evening. It began stirring in the early dawn, and Wade and Sloan stirred with it. Sloan scouted the trail taken by Spurlock's horse the night before, while Wade helped his family and the Wingates get loaded.

"Wanted to see where Spurlock went before everybody messed up the tracks with their horses," Sloan said when he got back. "He swung around and met somebody in the trees along the river west of town. They rode on together."

Wade nodded. "You know who that somebody was."

"Sure," Sloan said. "That means we'll have a lot better chance of catching Ardy. Two horses are easier to trail. And I don't figure Spurlock will be as good a rider or as tough as Ardy."

Wagons began rumbling out of town as families headed for Minneapolis. Wade helped lash the last things on the two wagons Jason and Vern Wingate were going to drive. The Wingates hadn't saved much from their home, so the Harpers had put some of their load in the Wingate wagon.

Feeling among the people was running high against the Orrs, and only a few had gone out to the new cemetery where they had buried Bradley Orr just at sunrise.

"I suppose you don't think Dack had a thing to do with the smuggling the Orrs were doing," Wade said to Jason before he climbed on his wagon to start out of town.

"I certainly don't," Jason said belligerently. "Herman would certainly never give the Indians guns."

"Where is he this morning?" Wade demanded.

"How do I know? Probably on the trail between here and Minneapolis, making sure it is safe for us to travel."

Wade turned away disgustedly. Catching Jennie as she left the house, he made one more try.

"Promise me you'll stay away from Dack, Jennie," he said earnestly.

"Why?" she asked angrily. "You've never showed

me any real proof that Herman is any of the things you say he is."

"I promise you, Jennie, that when I get hold of Ardy Orr I'll have proof. Just stay away from him till then."

"You'll never catch Ardy Orr," Jennie said. "He's part Indian, and after what he's done, you'd have to lick the whole Cheyenne nation to get to him."

"Maybe I'll do that," Wade said angrily. "But I'll bring the proof! Just stay away from Dack."

Wade saw the doubt in Jennie's eyes. She believed in Dack, but she couldn't question Wade's sincerity.

Wade turned to Martha, who was waiting to climb into the Wingate wagon. "Keep an eye on Jennie, will you, Martha?"

"Do you have to go after Ardy, Wade?" she asked, her hands on his arms.

Wade nodded. "He's got something that I must have. It's very important."

"More important than I?" she asked softly.

Wade's knees trembled. Why did she have to put it that way?

"I've got to go, Martha," he said. "Can't you see that?"

"Another killing won't bring the Bellings back to fe."

"It might save a lot more families like the Bellings." She bit her lip for a moment, then whirled and imbed into the wagon. With a heavy heart Wade atched the wagons start up the slope to the northeast. his wasn't the way he had hoped his parting with Iartha would be.

"We've got a lot of ground to cover, Wade," Red loan said as the wagons disappeared.

Wade whirled. He had forgotten Sloan. "I'm ready."

They picked up Ardy's trail close to the trees west of wn where two horses had met. The trail led out across e prairie, following no road, and within an hour, wung north. There they lost it.

"We'd better go by and bury Solly and the Bellings," Jade said. "Should have done it yesterday."

Sloan nodded. "Would have if we'd known the town as safe."

It was noon before their grim chore was completed. hen they rode north. For Ardy's trail had turned into e path taken by the raiders.

Wade puzzled over the problem of what Ardy was oing to do with Spurlock. Spurlock certainly wouldn't

join an Indian war party. If he did, some ambitiou
young buck would probably lift his scalp for a trophy
On the other hand, judging by the tracks back at Para
dise, Spurlock had ridden west of town for the expres
purpose of meeting Ardy. They must be traveling to
gether. Maybe Ardy wasn't going to join the Cheyenne:
But if he wasn't, where was he going?

They made camp that night on the open prairi
somewhere south of the Solomon. They had seen n
sign of Ardy or his companion. One burned homestea
was the only evidence they had found that Indians ha
come that way.

Dawn caught them in the saddle again. They reache
the Solomon, followed it as it curved southeast. A
Delphos, they found a few hardy men who had staye
when most had fled south to Minneapolis. They ha
seen no sign of a half-breed and a white man ridin
together.

"Those redskins will hightail it back toward thei
stomping grounds on the Washita now, I figure," Sloa
said as they left Delphos. "They won't stay up her
where the soldiers can get to them."

They set their course to the southwest again. Nigl
caught up with them on the open prairie once more.

As they rolled into their blankets, Wade voiced the
question that had been nagging him all afternoon:
"Are we just wasting our time?"

"Maybe," Sloan said with a sigh. "Our only real
hope is to catch Ardy before he joins up with the Indians. Once he's with them, we'll have to fight the whole
Cheyenne tribe to get him. I don't hanker for that job."

Morning found Wade and Sloan in the saddle again,
this time headed for Ft. Harker down on the Smoky
Hill River.

For nearly two days they hadn't seen anything that
they could be certain was the trail left by Ardy and
Spurlock. Then just before noon, they found proof that
they were on the right trail.

Wade saw it first, a bump on the prairie to his right.
He called Sloan's attention to it, and they rode that
way. Even though the white hair was gone, it wasn't
hard to recognize what was left of Sandy Spurlock.

"Looks like Indian work," Sloan said quietly.

"One Indian," Wade said. "Ardy Orr. Now he's free
to head straight for the Cheyennes."

Sloan nodded. "Likely. But he might stop at Ft.
Harker to find out all he can before going to the Indians."

Wade nodded. "Could be. He's just brazen enoug
to do that."

Sloan unbuckled the strap that held the short-har
dled spade behind his saddle. "It's a shame to depriv
the coyotes, but after all, he was a white man."

Wade followed suit. "Doesn't look like this hap
pened too long ago," he said. "Maybe we're not so fa
behind Ardy."

"We're not," Sloan agreed. "Let's finish this job an
get moving."

It was Wade's sharp eyes that again heralded a de
lay. It wasn't far from the spot where they had burie
Spurlock that Wade saw two poles standing boldly o
the prairie off to their right.

"What do you make of that?" he asked.

"No trees within miles of here," Sloan said. "There'
only one reason for poles being set out there like that
right on top of a hill, the hottest place on the prairie."

Wade nodded silently as he and Sloan reined to th
west toward the poles. Blind fury swept over him when
he saw the two women bound tightly to the stakes, lef
there to die of thirst and heat.

"I'll kill some of the red devils for this if I ever ge
the chance!" Wade said, fists clenched.

Sloan nodded grimly. "I'm going to make a chance. Wonder how long they've been dead."

Wade and Sloan dismounted. They decided the women had been dead for only a few hours. But they had been there for at least two days, maybe longer.

Wade had never known a hatred as fierce as the one that burned through his as he and Sloan cut the bodies free and buried them. The day would surely come when when he would have the chance to strike back at these fiends, and when it came, he'd not pass it up!

As a result of the delays caused by finding Spurlock and the two women, it was nearly noon the next day when Wade and Sloan rode into Ft. Harker.

Wade's horse had gone lame just a few miles from the fort, and Sloan had suggested they lay over for a while at the fort and see if they could pick up any news of Ardy.

Wade's first job after getting his horse taken care of was to inquire about Ardy. An hour of questions around the fort convinced him that Ardy had not been there.

Wade fretted through the days it took the veterinarian to rub the soreness out of his horse's leg with liniment. During that time he and Sloan waited hopefully for news that might give them a lead on Ardy.

When the news finally came, it took them by surprise. Wade and Sloan had gone into Ellsworth, about four miles from the fort. There they found a drummer who had just come in on the eastbound train from Hays City. He told of a store in Hays City that had been robbed a few days before by a heavy-set man who looked more Indian than white, although he spoke English.

Wade was sure that at last they had cut the trail of Ardy Orr. Probably by now he was miles from Hays City. But there at least they would be closer to him than at present.

Sunrise found them on the trail again, paralleling the rails of the Kansas Pacific railroad. In spite of the railroad, which was the mark of civilization in most people's minds, the country was as primitive and untamed as that west of Paradise.

Inquiry around Hays City and Ft. Hays, half a mile distant, revealed nothing that the drummer hadn't already told them. Wade was discouraged. It looked like the end of the trail.

"Ardy may have traded off that ring by now, anyway," Wade said dismally that night.

"I doubt it," Sloan said. "That half-breed likes flashy jewelry as well as any Indian who ever walked. Besides, he'll keep that ring to make Dack cough up the thousand when he kills you."

"Ardy's running in the wrong direction now if he intends to kill me. Besides, Dack's back east somewhere. Even if Ardy killed me, how would he collect?"

"Don't fool yourself. Ardy can find Dack when he wants to. And he'll want to if he can collect that thousand. You can bet he's sure you're on his trail. He knows now that you've figured out he killed Solly and will never rest till you've evened the score. If he can draw you out into his own country, he can kill you easily. That's how he'll figure. And after he kills you, he'll go back and collect from Dack."

Wade nodded.

"Where do we go from here?" he asked after a moment.

"Ft. Larned," Sloan said. "Ardy will probably go southwest toward the headquarters of his tribe. He might learn something about him at Larned."

Before heading south toward Ft. Larned, Wade and Sloan rode out to Ft. Hays the next morning.

They had planned to inquire about the country to

the south, feeling that the army could give them the best information about it. But there was news at the post that changed their plans.

A telegram had just come in on the wires up in Hays City and a messenger had brought it out to the fort. Orders had been received at Ft. Harker for Brevet Colonel George Forsyth to organize fifty volunteer scouts to take the trail of the Cheyenne warriors responsible for the recent raids and bring them to justice.

"Hear that?" Sloan shouted. "Here's where we get some action."

"We're after one man," Wade said: "Andy Orr."

"And where do you think he'll be?" Sloan countered.

"You said you thought he'd be down on the Washita with his tribe."

"If there's a war party of Cheyennes still up here on these plains, you can bet Ardy's with them," Sloan said. "If we join Forsyth, we'll get an escort on our hunt for Ardy. What could be better?"

Wade gave it a little thought and realized that Sloan was right. "I'm sold. We'll join Forsyth. But he's at Harker now."

"He'll be here," a sergeant standing nearby said. "He's to outfit here. He'll bring what men he can pick up at Harker. You can join him here if you want to go."

"We're going," Wade said.

XVI

As Colonel Forsyth's force rode out of the fort at sunup, Sloan nodded at the four-mule pack train bringing up the rear of the column.

"We're equipped to fight an army," he said. "They tell me there are camp kettles, salt and coffee, medicine, picks and shovels, and over four thousand rounds of ammunitions on those mules."

Wade nodded. "According to the scouts' reports, there are supposed to be a couple of hundred Cheyenne warriors that we're looking for out here."

"That's all right with me. There may be only fifty of us, but we'll sure show two hundred redskins how the cat licked his ear."

Wade shared Sloan's confidence if not his enthusiasm.

The column swung north away from Ft. Hays with all the vigor and spirit of a conquering army. At the column's head rode Colonel George A. Forsyth with the proud bearing of a true officer in the U. S. Cavalry. The efficiency with which he had organized and equipped his little company revealed the determination and purpose that had made him ask for the command.

They reached the Saline River and camped. The search through the valley of the Solomon and the tributaries of the Republican River brought nothing other than sign on Beaver Creek, where some sort of powwow had been held. A sun dance, said Jack Stillwell, a fuzzy-cheeked boy of eighteen, studying the sign. In spite of Stillwell's youth, no one questioned his opinion.

"It took a lot of Indians to make that," Sloan said.

"Sign's old," Stillwell said. "These Indians are probably a long way from here by now."

Forsyth turned his column south and west.

They had been out of Ft. Hays a little over a week when they came down into the valley of the south fork of the Smoky Hill River. There, where the tiny little stream called Pond Creek ran into the Smoky Hill, was Ft. Wallace.

"We've been out here a week," Wade said as he and Sloan bedded down for the night, "and I'm no closer to Ardy than I was."

"Oh, you're closer, all right," Sloan said. "Ardy's somewhere this side of Ft. Hays. Just where is the question."

"Think Forsyth will quit now?"

Sloan shook his head. "He hasn't started yet. I figure he's as stubborn as a mule. He came out here to find those Cheyennes, and he'll stay till he does."

Wade thought of the endless prairies. A man or an army could spend a year out there and never see anything but prairie dogs and rattlesnakes and an occasional herd of antelope or buffalo.

"How about the men? Think they want to go on?"

"There are no quitters in this company," Sloan said. "Remember, most of them come from Lincoln and Ottawa Counties, same as we do. They've got a score to settle with those murdering redskins. They came to fight. They'd be mighty unhappy if they didn't get to do it."

Wade agreed. He thought of Lt. Fred Beecher, second in command to Col. Forsyth. Lt. Beecher shared his colonel's determination to punish the Cheyennes. He was no new hand in battle. He walked with a limp, a reminder of Gettysburg. The company had a fine doctor, too, a necessity on a campaign such as this. Wade had heard some men talking about him just a couple of nights before. Dr. J. H. Mooers, an army surgeon, had been a major in the New York Volunteers during the war. Then there was Sergeant William H. H. McCall who had commanded a Pennsylvania regiment at Petersburg, Virginia. None of those men, Wade knew, was ready to quit.

"How long will we lay over here?" Wade asked.

"Not long, I'd guess," Sloan said. "We'll get supplies for another week and try again. Now get to sleep or you'll be in the saddle before you're awake."

Wade wondered the next morning if Sloan was a prophet. The men were routed out before dawn and given the boots and saddle call.

"What's up?" Wade asked as he reined his horse into the column that was rapidly forming on the parade ground.

"Indians raided a freighter over at Sheridan, the way I get it," Sloan said. "Killed two drivers. This may be what we've been looking for."

"More dead men?"

"A hot trail," Sloan said.

The little company moved out of Ft. Wallace before it was fully light.

Sheridan was a tiny outpost at the end of steel where the Kansas Pacific railroad had paused momentarily to catch its breath on its push across the prairie to the mountains. The Indians were gone, but their trail was fresh and clear, and Forsyth led his column north on that trail.

Wade hoped they might overtake the Indians and force the battle early. But that hope faded as the miles slipped behind and they didn't see a single red-skinned warrior.

Then the trail split. Even Sharp Grover, the company's chief scout, with eyes like an eagle, could only point in the three directions in which the Indians had gone after breaking into small parties.

Forsyth led his men on the trail that ran straight ahead. But the days passed and hope faded. Then, when they reached a good-sized stream, Forsyth called a halt.

"Think this is the end?" Wade asked Sloan.

Sloan rubbed his chin as he studied the little knot of men at the head of the column. Forsyth and Beecher were there, listening attentively to Sharp Grover and the blue-eyed youngster with the light hair, Jack Still-well.

"Looks like we're going on," Sloan said after a moment. "We're on the Republican. But if we don't find sign pretty quick, my guess is we'll have to give up."

"Still in Kansas?"

Sloan shrugged. "I'm not much of a map reader. I think we're in the southwest corner of Nebraska now. But Indians are Indians wherever we find them. And I hope we find these pretty soon."

Then, when hope seemed almost dead, they found an abandoned wickiup on the banks of the Republican. Two Indians had been there recently, Sharp Grover reported.

Excitement spread down the line of mounted men, and they pushed forward. They found another abandoned camp, this one fresher than the first. Three Indians had been there, Grover said.

By noon the next day, they had come on more camps; each time, the Indians who had left had gone west up the Republican. Now, Grover estimated, they were trailing upwards of twenty Indians.

Enthusiasm was at a fever pitch when they reached a fork of the river where another tributary came in.

Here the trail turned southwest up this tributary: the Arickaree River, one scout said.

This trail, in contrast to the one that had gradually faded out north of Ft. Wallace, became plainer with every mile.

"More Indians," Wade said, looking ahead.

"A lot more," Sloan agreed ominously.

But still there was no real alarm in the column; only an increasing alertness. Every man knew now that they were trailing more than a hundred Indians. The odds had gone over to the side of the redskins.

Then at noon the next day they came to a junction of trails.

Sharp Grover reported to Forsyth in a voice that Wade could barely hear, "Fresh."

"How many would you say?"

"Can't tell. Hundreds. Maybe a thousand. Maybe even more. Got their families along, too. See the marks of the travois?"

"That will make them easier to overtake," Forsyth said.

"Too easy, maybe," Grover said.

Wade looked at Sloan. "Do we go back?" He kept his voice low. No one was shouting any more.

Sloan shook his head. "We've come too far now."

Up ahead, the colonel seemed to agree with Sloan. Forsyth apparently had come to fight Indians, and he intended to do just that regardless of the odds.

XVII

Gray mist shrouded the valley in a prelude to dawn when Wade awoke, the sentry's cry of "Indians" piercing his sleep. He was on his feet instantly, his Spencer in his hand.

For a moment he saw and heard nothing. Then the air was filled with howls and yells, and Wade saw the raiders sweeping down on the camp.

The next two minutes were ones of confusion. Although Wade had never been in an Indian battle, he could see that the purpose of this first charge was not to annihilate the camp but to stampede the horses.

Wade was thankful that Forsyth had insisted on every man making doubly sure his picket pin was securely driven into the sod the night before. As a result only a few of the horses and mules broke free.

Wade was on one knee, Sloan beside him, pumping bullets at the dim figures bobbing around on the horses. The gray light was still too weak to allow accurate shooting, and the result was that the first skirmish netted little for either side.

Then the Indians were gone and each man was checking his horse. Wade heard one man say to a companion. "We showed them something that time." His only reply was, "Load that rifle."

Wade had never saddled so quickly as he did in the growing light there by the Arickaree. The surrounding hills were visible now, but Wade didn't take time to look around until he heard a gasp from Sloan.

"Take a look, Wade. A thousand of them."

Wade turned slowly. The hills to the north were lined like a picket fence with mounted Indians. The valley to the west was full of them. And to the south, across the flat plain leading to the hills, another line of mounted Indians was bearing down on them.

For an awful moment, Wade felt that he couldn't move. Sloan's estimate of a thousand Indians was low, he was sure. There must be three thousand out there. He could see them rising out of the grass now at close range. What had been a silent prairie in the early light was suddenly transformed into a horde of howling savages, racing forward in wild anticipation of the scalps they would soon take.

Wade came out of his trance and whirled to the east. Downstream there were no Indians. Although they were pouring in on three sides, there was still one lane of escape. He wheeled to Forsyth for the command to mount and dash downstream to safety.

Forsyth, with Grover standing beside him, gave his command, but it killed the faint hope of escape that had flickered momentarily in Wade.

"To the island! Hitch your horses!"

There was a wild scramble. Horses and men charged through the shallow water of the little stream to an island in the center of the river.

Wade had noticed the island the night before but had paid little attention to it. It was almost exactly in the middle of the river and the highest elevation couldn't have been over two or three feet above the water. It was about sixty yards long and perhaps twenty feet wide. It was covered with grass. There were some wild plum bushes and willow shrubs. A lone cottonwood tree stood in the middle of the island.

The island was about fifty yards from the south bank

of the river bed, but the stream was low now and wasn't over five or six yards wide where it flowed next to the island. The horses barely got their feet wet splashing through it.

Forsyth and Grover must have known instinctively that the narrow valley they had come through yesterday just before camping would be a death trap. Those hills crowded in close to the river. They would make a perfect ambush. The Indians wouldn't overlook that. They had left the eastern side of their trap open for a reason.

But the wild dash to the island, although completely upsetting the strategy of the Indians, also meant some losses for the soldiers. The Indians who had sneaked up on foot during the night and had appeared as if by magic at morning now used their rifles as they saw what the whites were doing.

Somehow the mules, laden with rations and medical supplies, were all lost. But most of the men reached the island with their horses and dropped from their saddles, quickly tying the horses in the bushes.

The war cries of the Indians changed to shouts of wild rage as they realized they had been frustrated in their ambush. But it didn't dampen their determination to wipe out the little band of invaders.

Wade and Sloan were side by side as they hit the sand of the island. The grass was thin here, apparently having taken root since the last flood had swept over the island. Grabbing his butcher knife, Wade cut through the thin sod and found soft sand underneath. Using his tin plate for a scoop, he began hollowing out a pit. Sloan was digging like a badger just to Wade's left.

But they had little time to dig. Down from the hills to the north and across the flat land to the south the Indians were coming at breakneck speed. Bullets began splattering into the island, and arrows whistled through the air and buried themselves in the sand.

Wade glanced about quickly. The men were crouching around the island. Not a one had fired a shot. They were waiting, every rifle loaded to its limit of seven shells. It seemed to Wade that the howling warriors were almost on them before a rifle spoke.

Then every rifle came to life, and the front row of painted bodies were mowed off their horses like grass before a scythe. Screams of agony mingled with the war cries.

Volley after volley came from the island, and screams of pain and wild rage swelled above the battle cries. From the top of the hills to the north, a thousand women and children had gathered to watch their warriors take fifty scalps. Now their wails and screams added to the bedlam.

The charge broke, going by on either side of the island. Many warriors turned back to pick up their dead.

Wade had no illusions of victory when the Indians withdrew after this first charge. They would be back, and they would be much better organized.

Not a man on the island needed to be told to dig his pit deeper. But that wasn't easy to do. The tall grass on either bank of the stream was filled now with Indian riflemen who were remarkably accurate with their weapons. Any man who raised his head above the grass was inviting a ticket to the next world.

Wade and Sloan, using their tin plates, lowered their pits until they were deep enough to feel safe from the snipers on the bank. Wade tried to keep his mind on the fortress of sand he was throwing up around his pit and not to listen to the screams of the horses as the Indians methodically picked them off. When the last horse went down, there was a lull in the firing and Wade heard a voice yell in clear English:

"There goes the last horse."

Wade shot a glance across at Sloan to see if he had heard. Sloan was looking at him.

"Maybe they don't all have red skins out there."

Wade nodded. He couldn't help thinking of Ardy.

The firing from the river banks slackened as the men on the island dug their pits deep enough so that they no longer made targets for the hidden marksmen.

Low voices around the island pieced together the story of how the company had survived the first charge. The picture wasn't bright. The army surgeon, Dr. J. H. Mooers, had received a serious wound and was already out of his head. He couldn't help the other wounded men, who needed him badly. Forsyth himself had been shot in both legs and couldn't move around. Two or three men were dead and over a dozen wounded, some so seriously that they couldn't help with the fighting.

Sloan slipped out of his pit and wriggled like a snake over to a man who was never going to need a rifle again. Getting the rifle and ammunition, he wriggled back into his pit beside Wade.

"Thought we might be able to use another loaded rifle pretty soon. They don't give us much time to reload."

"Think their next try will be worse?"

"Bound to be." Sloan turned his head to the north, then to the south. "Notice the firing has almost stopped? I don't like that."

Wade didn't like anything about the situation. The sun was beginning to burn down on the men: the dead, the dying, and those waiting to be killed. Wade had no hope of seeing the sun that night. The one purpose left in life for the men trapped on that little world of sand was to set the price on their lives as high as possible.

"Look there, Red," Wade said softly, pointing to a high bluff.

Indian horsemen were gathering on the bluff, hundreds of them. Sunlight flashed from rifles.

Then the horsemen filed down off the bluff and took their positions in the valley below the island, well out of rifle range. The snipers along the banks of the river increased their fire until no man on the island dared lift his head for a better view downstream.

Then the Indians moved forward like a huge avalanche. First they came at a trot, then at a gallop. As far as Wade could see, not one rider got out of line. They charged, sixty men abreast, six or eight ranks deep, the thunder of their horses' hoofs mingling with shrieks of encouragement from the women and children on the hills to the north.

In the lead was an Indian of whom Wade had heard:
Roman Nose.

Each warrior was streaked with bright paint until he
looked more like something out of a hideous nightmare
than a human being. He was completely naked except
for his cartridge belt and box and moccasins. The warriors rode bareback, with horsehair lariats wrapped
around the middle of their horses and looped over each
knee. Those who weren't wearing war bonnets had their
hair braided, their scalp locks decorated with feathers.
They held their reins in their left hands and their rifles
in their right.

Even in all the furor, with the tension threatening
to snap his nerves, Wade found his attention gripped
by the magnificent picture of Roman Nose. A giant of
a man, measuring well over six feet, he towered above
the warriors he led. On his head was the grandest war
bonnet Wade had ever seen. Two black buffalo horns
curved just above his brow, and the bonnet fell away
behind him, a long streamer of eagle and heron feathers. He wore moccasins and a blood red sash around
his waist and nothing else. He had tremendously broad
shoulders, and he held his rifle in the crook of his left

arm while his left hand gripped the horse's mane and the rein. His right hand directed the warriors on to the attack.

Every man in Forsyth's command had turned to face the foot of the island and the charge but not a shot was fired as they waited. The snipers on the banks kept up a steady fire until it seemed to Wade that the charge was almost upon the island. Then the snipers stopped firing, and Forsyth's order rang out.

"Now!"

The first volley cut a wide path in the center of the front rank of Indians. But still Roman Nose, at the head of the center column, and the medicine man who was leading the left column, stayed on their mounts. The second and third volley from the men on the island failed to crack the concentrated charge. The cries from the hills now turned to shrieks of rage, but still Roman Nose led his warriors on.

Wade was firing his rifle with a calmness he would never have guessed he possessed under such circumstances. The end of the charge seemed inevitable. Fifty men, no matter how perfect their marksmanship, could never stop four or five hundred warriors in a perfectly organized charge such as this.

Then the fourth volley cut down the medicine man. Still Roman Nose rode erect, sweeping through the water, almost to the edge of the island itself now. The war cries had stopped; each warrior was concentrating on firing his rifle as he rode, saving his energy for the last minute hand-to-hand fighting that would end the battle.

Wade lost count of the bullets he had fired, but knew his rifle must be almost empty. Roman Nose would be on the island in another second or two. The ranks behind him had closed in until the first warriors were close behind their leader.

The next volley of bullets from the island seemed to do little damage to the main ranks of the Indians. Every man apparently was determined to cut down the great Cheyenne leader. Both Roman Nose and his horse went down under the volley.

Two warriors caught their leader and whirled toward the bank of the stream. The charge came on, but the next volley from the scouts broke it, and the warriors faltered, swinging to either side of the island.

Wade's rifle was empty. Like half the men on the island, he leaped out of his pit and raced to meet the Indians, firing his revolver.

But the charge was over. The Indians broke ranks and scurried for the banks on either side of the river. Wade wheeled and dashed back to his pit. As soon as the warriors were out of the river, the snipers on the banks would open up again.

But the scouts were all back in their pits before the snipers fired another shot. Shrieks and wailing from the bluffs north of the river filled the valley.

"They'll never be able to do better than that," Sloan said as he settled wearily back in his pit.

"Neither will we," Wade said.

He was loading his rifle again when word came down the line that Lt. Fred Beecher had been killed. Now their commander was wounded, almost helpless, and his lieutenant dead. The doctor was dying. Nearly half the men were unable to fight. Their medicine and food supplies were gone. Even though the best the Cheyennes could do had been repulsed and Roman Nose killed, it was a bleak outlook that faced the scouts on the island.

The sun bore down with blistering heat, and the wounded cried for water. A man named Burke close to Wade dug his pit down to water and filled his canteen. The water was muddy, but it was wet and cool, and the canteen made several trips from hand to hand, quenching thirsts as the day wore on.

There was another charge by the Indians in mid-afternoon, but it was mild and impotent compared to the well organized charge directed by Roman Nose in the forenoon.

At evening the Indians tried again and came nearer success than they had in the morning, not because of their organization but because of the weakness of the defenders. Some of the warriors got on the island this time. But once again the main body was split and scattered, and the few Indians who got their feet on the island didn't live to brag about it.

Still it seemed to Wade that they had succeeded only in postponing the inevitable. He had never felt so discouraged or helpless as when he watched the sun disappear into the clouds that promised rain during the night.

XVIII

The rain came, soft and gentle. It cooled the fever of the wounded and refreshed the spirits of the battle weary. Never had Wade felt anything more welcome.

"Let's use these butcher knives," Sloan said as the rain fell. "Horse meat won't be such bad fare."

Wade said nothing as he climbed out of his pit and went with Sloan to the dead horses. Other men were already there. In an hour the bushes were covered with slabs of horse meat.

"We'll let it dry in the sun tomorrow," Sloan said. "It will keep longer that way."

"Just how long do you think we'll be here?" Wade asked.

"Not too long," Sloan said. "Or else forever."

The men gathered around the pit they had dug for

their commander. Forsyth, wounded in both legs and suffering from a bad scalp wound, still was able to think rationally and direct the plans.

They talked of sending out for relief, but the general conclusion was that a messenger would have no chance. They also had to consider the torture that the messenger would be subjected to if caught by the Indians.

But when the discussion had ended, Jack Stillwell calmly volunteered to make the effort if someone would go with him. A man named Pierre Trudeau unhesitatingly said he'd go. Forsyth gave them his blessing.

Wade watched them prepare for their attempt to slip through the Indians. They took off their boots, hung them around their necks and wrapped themselves in blankets. Then, about midnight, they stole off the island, saying they would walk backward in their stocking feet to leave tracks like moccasins pointed toward the island.

"How long will it take if they get through?" Sloan asked as they disappeared.

"Grover figures about six days to get relief back from Ft. Wallace," Wade said.

"Six days," Sloan said. "What will they find when they get back here?"

The men spent most of the rest of the night improving their pits and connecting them with trenches so they could crawl back and forth.

Dawn brought the heat back. The valley steamed after the shower of the night before, and the day promised to be blisteringly hot again. The breakfast menu was raw horse meat. If Wade hadn't been so hungry, he couldn't have gotten it down. But he gulped it, washing it down with muddy water from Burke's deep pit.

The Indians kept up their sniping from the grass along the river banks, but there were no more concentrated charges like the one Roman Nose had led the day before.

"Figure on starving us out," Sloan said.

"Or picking us off if we get careless," Wade added.

"Might be better than starving, at that."

At noon, when the horse meat was beginning to dry, Wade and Sloan crawled out of their pits and pulled their meat off the bushes, drawing fire from the snipers meanwhile. They dug pits close by and buried the meat deep in the sand. If they could have gotten it completely cured in the sun, it would have kept longer. But the flies were swarming around it, and they decided the sand was the best place for it.

In the heat of mid-afternoon, even the snipers slackened off in their firing, and Wade dozed in his pit. He was wakened suddenly by a yell. It came from the north river bank, and it was in English.

"Like it out there?"

Wade jerked upright, and only Sloan's quick hand grabbing his arm kept him from rearing up for a look.

"You sure fell for that," Sloan said.

"That sounded like Ardy," Wade said.

Sloan agreed. "It did, at that. But what good is that going to do you?"

"He couldn't know I'm here," Wade said.

"Couldn't he?" Every redskin that wanted a look at us got it before we ever got into this fix. You know they were watching us from the time we left the Republican."

Wade nodded. He hadn't considered that. If Ardy Orr was with these Indians, he would surely have scouted Forsyth's command to see if he knew any of the men. Nothing would please Ardy more than to torture Wade. And letting Wade know he was out there, just beyond reach, was the perfect way to do it.

Wade finally decided that Ardy, if it was Ardy, must think that he had been killed in the early fighting, for no more taunts came from the bank.

Then, just at sundown, the voice came again. It was still in the same spot.

"You'll rot out there. Come on and fight."

This time Wade wasn't tempted to jump up for a look. He peeped over the sand he had piled around his pit to get a fixed location on the voice. An idea was brewing in his mind.

"That sounds like Ardy, all right," Sloan said.

Wade nodded grimly.

"Only reason I can think of for Ardy wanting you to know he's out there," Sloan said, "is to get you to show yourself so he can plug you. He'd get paid for that."

"You figure he still plans to hold Dack to that agreement?"

"You can bet he does. And he'll collect, too, if he kills you. Even Dack wouldn't dare cross him by refusing to pay."

Darkness settled over the valley. The men gathered around their commander for another conference. Two more men volunteered to try to get through to Ft. Wallace. The chances that Stillwell and Trudeau had gotten through were too slim to stir hope in any of the men.

The new volunteers prepared themselves and waited until almost midnight before moving silently away from the island.

Wade watched with the other men as they left; then he slipped back to his own pit. Sloan had been engrossed in watching the two scouts leave and didn't miss Wade.

Wade propped his rifle up in the pit. Holding the revolver in his hand, he debated for a minute before laying it down beside the rifle. He'd have no use for it on his mission. Silence would be everything. Taking the butcher knife they had issued him back at Ft. Hays, he crawled out of his pit and slipped quietly through the bushes to the edge of the water.

Clouds were over the sky now, clouds that would have been most welcome during the heat of the day. They were still welcome to Wade, for they pulled the inky darkness in tightly around him. Before dark, from the safety of his sand pit, he had marked indelibly in his mind the bush next to the water where he would leave the island. His sense of direction would have to carry him from there.

He crawled through the water, which was no more than eight or ten inches deep anywhere and only a few yards wide. Then he had to cross the long stretch of sand. Maybe he would lose his way. Or maybe Ardy the tall grass that grew along the bank.

Misgivings assailed Wade as he inched across the sand. Maybe he would lose his way. Or maybe Ardy was gone. Would Ardy spend the night where he had spent the day? It was a long chance, but one Wade had to take.

The bank of the creek suddenly loomed ahead of him, reaching two feet above the level of the sandy river bed. The grass standing two feet high on the bank made Wade feel he was facing a four-foot wall.

If Wade had guessed right and crawled straight, he should now be just a few feet upstream from the spot where Ardy had been that afternoon. As silently as a snake he pulled himself up the bank and into the grass.

For a minute he lay motionless, trying to smother his heavy breathing. There was no sound around him. But that didn't quiet the thumping of his heart. He knew from the experience he had had in tracking Indians that the less sign you saw the more alert you had to be.

Convinced at last that no enemy eyes or ears had noted his arrival on the bank, he began moving cautiously through the grass. If his calculations were right and if Ardy hadn't moved, he should be within a few feet of him now.

Something moved the grass just ahead of him and he stopped, every muscle rigid. It might be an animal. But the only animals he had noticed were coyotes. Those scavengers had been attracted by the scent of death that permeated the valley, and they filled the night air with their howls of hunger and frustration. But they seldom moved in close, for their sharp noses detected the presence of their mortal enemy, man, along with the enticing odor of decaying flesh.

It wasn't a coyote ahead of Wade. No coyote would have allowed a man to come that close to him. It had to be a man. But was it Ardy?

Wade moved ahead; he had to rely on his conviction that Ardy would eat and sleep right where he was so that he would not miss any opportunity to carry out his threat to kill Wade.

The inky blackness allowed only a few feet of vision even to eyes accustomed to it. Wade saw the man an instant before some intuition made him turn. Wade couldn't be sure even then that it was Ardy. But he leaped forward as the man brought around his rifle.

Wade knocked the rifle spinning, bringing his knife around in the same motion. But the other man reacted like a flash, dodging to one side, whipping a knife from somewhere beneath him.

Wade was on him then, and he saw that he had guessed right. This was Ardy Orr. But he had no time to exult over his success in finding Ardy. Ardy was a powerful man, and now that Wade had knocked his rifle off into the darkness, they each had one weapon, a knife.

The advantage was with Ardy now that his surprise was over. Ardy would be more accustomed to wielding a knife with intent to kill. And if their battle was noisy, Indian reinforcements could be expected.

The thought of the torture that would await him if he were captured passed only momentarily through Wade's mind. He concentrated every fiber of his being on the battle at hand.

Ardy had rolled away from Wade, and now he swung his knife. Wade dodged back, unable to see the blade but hearing it hiss through the air. He brought his butcher knife around in a sweep, hoping to catch Ardy before he recovered. But Ardy struck his arm, and the knife went flying into the grass.

Wade dodged back, knowing that now he was at the mercy of Ardy. But Ardy didn't press forward, and Wade realized he didn't know that Wade's knife was gone.

The cloud cover above broke just a little, letting a faint light seep down into the valley. Wade made out Ardy, crouching like a panther. As Ardy saw Wade, he sprang forward, bringing the knife around in a slashing sweep.

Wade dodged back, barely escaping the knife. Then he leaped forward, catching Ardy's arm and bringing his knee up under it with a jerk. He felt the blade of the knife rip into the fleshy part of his thigh. But Ardy's grip on the knife was broken and the knife slithered away into the grass.

Time was running out on Wade. He and Ardy were on even terms again, but the noise their fight was making was sure to bring other Indians to investigate.

Wade leaped forward, gripping Ardy in a wrestling hold. This was just what Ardy wanted, he knew. But Wade had to get hold of Ardy, to pull him out into the river where they could finish their fight in private.

The force of Wade's charge carried both men over the bank. Only when they crashed onto the sandy river

ed below did Ardy put up any resistance to the rolling
ght.

He drove hard fists into Wade's ribs, making breath-
ng painful for Wade. But Wade was now intent on
etting Ardy far out into the river bed, away from the
ank. As Ardy drew back a fist to slam it into Wade's
ibs again, Wade lurched away and rolled toward the
enter of the river bed.

As Wade expected, Ardy leaped after him. They
ere almost to the edge of the water when they came
o grips again. Now they were closer to the island than
he river bank, and Wade felt he had eliminated the
hance of Ardy's Indian confederates coming to his aid.
Now neither side would dare shoot for fear of hitting
ts own man. And neither side was liable to send out
couts to find out what was going on. Scouts would
nly offer targets to the enemy in case the clouds should
reak.

Exhaustion was beginning to overcome Wade, slow-
ng his actions and taking some of the strength from
is arms. Ardy seemed to be gripped by a frenzy of
ate, and his strength was gradually wearing Wade
own. They rolled into the edge of the water, where
Ardy came out on top. Wade realized he was facing his

last minutes of life unless he did something soon.

Drawing back his fist for a blow at Ardy's face, Wade's hand dipped into the water and hit against a rock. His fingers closed on it. It wasn't big, but it felt heavy in his hand. He slammed the rock against the side of Ardy's head, and for a moment the half-breed wavered.

Wade summoned all his strength and heaved upward, upsetting Ardy. He leaped on him, and in a matter of seconds, the situation of a minute before was reversed.

Wade managed to get Ardy's arm pinned under his knees and struggled to hold them there. Ardy's strength was beginning to wane, weakened perhaps by that blow on his head. Realizing that, Wade took new courage and bore down on his arms, keeping them pinned to the sand.

Suddenly Ardy relaxed, a sign of surrender. But Wade wasn't fooled. Ardy, he knew, would never surrender. Then for the first time, Ardy used his tongue.

"What good is this going to do you?"

"You've got that ring Dack gave you. I want it."

"It won't do you any good. You're fighting Dack because of your sister and that Wingate girl. But you left him alone with them."

A chill ran over Wade. His fingers touched Ardy's throat. "What do you mean?"

"Dack bragged he'd marry Jennie whether she liked it or not. And he'd have Martha, too. You can't stop him now."

A wave of helplessness swept over Wade. He didn't doubt the truth of Ardy's words. And here he was hundreds of miles away, pinned down by a thousand Indians, while Dack probably had free rein over everything he wanted back in eastern Kansas.

Ardy, taking advantage of Wade's shock, exploded all his strength and shoved Wade back, then lunged to his feet. Wade leaped up, realizing the trick Ardy had used on him, his feeling of helplessness erupting into a frenzy of hate. If it hadn't been for Ardy, he wouldn't have been there now. He would have been back in Minneapolis or Paradise protecting Jennie and Martha from Herman Dack. Wade was consumed with the desire to pound Ardy to a pulp.

Ardy was willing to exchange blows, but his great strength was no match for the fury inside Wade. Gradually Wade drove him back. Finally Ardy lunged forward, grabbing Wade around the waist.

They went down again, and Wade was once more at a disadvantage. But Wade kept himself from being pinned down. He rolled, winding up in the water. Ardy caught him with a first, and Wade felt as if the side of his head were caving in. Dimly he realized that Ardy had a rock in his hand now. With all his strength, he threw himself at Ardy just as Ardy was setting himself for another blow.

Ardy, confident he had taken the fight out of Wade with that blow, was caught off balance and went down in the water under Wade's weight. He landed face down, and Wade used all his strength to hold him there.

For a minute there was a terrific battle; then Ardy's struggles became weaker and ended. Wade rolled back on the sand, exhausted. He wasn't sure how long he rested, but clouds still blackened the sky when he regained enough strength to move.

Slowly he dragged Ardy's body through the water to the edge of the island. There he took the leather pouch that he found swinging on a thong around Ardy's neck. Wade went through the pockets of the pants Ardy was wearing and felt of each finger, but found nothing. If Ardy had kept the ring, it had to be in the pouch.

Slowly he made his way back toward his pit in the sand. His mind was too tired and dull to think of anything except that he had been a fool to come out there and leave Dack running free.

XIX

"Where have you been?" Sloan demanded the instant Wade dropped into his pit.

"After Orr," Wade said.

"Get him?"

"Yeah."

"Good. Did he have the ring on him?"

Wade slumped down wearily. "I don't know. He had a leather pouch. I got it. Have to wait until it's light to see what's in it."

Sloan said no more, and Wade dropped into a fitful sleep, complete exhaustion claiming him.

He woke at dawn to the snap of snipers' bullets. His hand still gripped the leather pouch, and he opened it as soon as he had roused enough to think clearly.

There were several rings with brilliant stones, a

couple of jeweled breastpins and some gold coins. Then he saw it, a ring with a stone twice as big as any other. Wade would have known it anywhere. That was the one Dack had been flashing around so proudly.

If Jennie could see this ring now, she'd believe what Wade had told her about Dack.

"It was there, was it?" Sloan asked.

Wade stared at the ring. "Now what do I do with it?"

"We've got a few Indians to lick before you do anything."

Wade looked at his rifle and the dwindling supply of ammunition. "Did the boys who went out last night get through?"

"Came back in about three o'clock. Said there's no way through."

"That means Stillwell and Trudeau didn't make it?"

"Maybe. Maybe not. We've got to hope they did."

Hope was fading fast for the survivors on the island. It would have been easy to abandon it completely, but it was the only thing left for them. The fiery zeal for revenge that had sparked the men when they had left Ft. Hays an eternity ago was gone now, and there remained only a consuming hunger for escape and rest.

The day was cloudy, and for that Wade was thank-

ful. At noon the Indian women and children disappeared from the hills, and the valley grew quiet except
for the occasional snap of a sniper's rifle.

"Going to starve us till we can't fight, then move in
for the kill," Sloan said.

Wade thought of the horse meat down in the sand,
already beginning to spoil. "It won't take long."

Darkness saw another conference around the pit
where Col. Forsyth lay. Two more men, Donovan and
Pliley, volunteered to try to make it through to Ft. Wallace. Everyone knew this was the last chance. If they
didn't make it, there would be no point in trying again.
Even if someone got through later, there would be no
one to rescue by the time he brought back help.

Col. Forsyth sent a complete report with the two
scouts, and they slipped out into the night, much as the
others had done.

The men on the island waited through the night, but
Donovan and Pliley didn't come back. However, no
man there took it for granted that they had succeeded
in getting past the Indians. They might be dead, or perhaps they had been captured and were undergoing
some fiendish torture.

The day dragged on. In the afternoon when Wade

dug up his horse meat, he found it so putrid he couldn't stand the smell of it close to his nose, much less attempt to eat it.

"Looks like we live on our imagination from here on," Sloan said.

"Suppose we could put enough gunpowder on it we could eat it?"

Sloan eyed the meat dubiously. "Maybe. But I'll have to be a little farther gone than I am now to do it."

Shortly after dark, temptation overcame caution in a coyote, and he came out into the river bed, leaped the narrow stream and prepared to feast on the dead horses, which had been enticing him for so long. A marksman in a pit close to the horse the coyote chose cut him down with one shot.

Every man able to eat had a small portion of fresh meat then, and soup was made from the bones of the greedy animal. The meat wasn't good, but no man turned it down.

Wade sank down in the pit, the gnawing hunger in him creating illusions of tables full of food. Through the stench of decaying flesh that seemed to thicken the air came a clear memory of the aroma of freshly baked bread. As a boy, Wade had waited eagerly at his mother's side while she lifted steaming hot loaves from the oven and turned them out of the pan. Then he'd get the crust off one end of a loaf and watch the freshly churned butter melt on it. He would be eating it while it was still so hot it almost burned his mouth.

Twice during the night, Wade roused as he was climbing out of his pit to get some of that hot bread his mother seemed to be holding out to him. Each time he sank back deeper in despair.

Days and nights became one long nightmare. The only difference between them was that the hot glaring sun beat down during the day, whereas the long nights seemed to get chillier each time they closed in.

The snipers fired less and less and finally not at all. Wade wondered vaguely if they were gone or just waiting for some foolish fellow to rise up to see.

On the sixth night on the island, if Wade hadn't lost count of the long days and nights, they held another meeting around the sand pit where Forsyth lay, wounded but still clear of mind.

"Think they're gone, Colonel?" one man asked.

"No. Just waiting."

"They know we'll starve," Sloan said. "Why should they waste any more bullets on us?"

"They're back in the hills where they don't have to boil in the sun all day," another said. "We could make a run for Ft. Wallace—those of us who are able."

Silence fell over the men. Only about two dozen were without wounds that would force them to stay here. Wade was one of those. But somehow, as badly as he wanted to get away from the place, he couldn't get excited at the thought of escape while leaving the wounded to suffer their final hours at the hands of those fiendish devils.

Wade doubted if many of the Indians were still around. Most of them had surely moved on. But there were enough there to assure the maximum of torture for any white man they got their hands on. With the battle so nearly won, they wouldn't leave without the final victory.

The suggestion of escape for those able to walk was making a great impression on the unwounded, Wade saw. They were gaunt men with hollow cheeks and sunken eyes, their faces grown over with heavy beards, their clothes torn and dirty, hanging like sacks from their shriveled frames. But the spark of hope and life was still there, fanned now by the possibility of escape.

It would be a dangerous undertaking. But certainly

they would have a much better chance of getting through than the scouts who had gone out at the beginning of the siege. The Indians lurking in the hills, waiting, might not even discover that half of the men were gone. If they did, their pursuit would be quick and the end merciless. But it was a chance. The men had none if they stayed here.

One man, on the far side of the circle from Wade, spoke up, voicing Wade's feelings better than he could have himself.

"We fought together. I say, let's die together if we have to."

A murmur of agreement ran slowly around the circle. Every man there, Wade was certain, felt that he would die if he stayed. Hope that either of the two teams of messengers who had gone out had gotten through was rapidly fading. Yet they were voting to stay.

Wade felt better when the meeting broke up and each man sought a place to try to rest. It hadn't brought him any nearer escape; in fact, it had sealed the fate of all the men, it seemed to him. But they wouldn't be leaving the wounded. That was as it should be.

They had known when they came on this campaign

that they might not come back, although Wade doubted if there had been a man in the group who hadn't been confident he personally would make it. Wade had had his own selfish reasons for coming, in addition to his desire to punish the Cheyennes for the massacres along the Smoky Hill, Saline and Solomon Rivers. He had accomplished that selfish mission when he had gotten the ring from Ardy. But what good was it going to do him now?

Two more days wore by. Not a sniper fired a shot at the island. Wade, with four other men, forded the creek and scouted around the area close to the island for anything that could be used for food. They were not molested by Indians. Yet the sharp eyes of some of the scouts on the island saw the Indians watching from the hills to the north. They were there, waiting. If the men attempted to leave, they would descend on them like eagles pouncing on their prey. But they had had enough of trying to roust them out of their stronghold on the island.

A few wild plums were all that the foraging party could bring back. And those were found on the bushes at one end of the island. The stewed plums were welcomed eagerly as they were doled out carefully to each man.

But there wasn't enough food to stave off the weakness that stole over each man as the hours dragged by. By the ninth day, Wade was sure the Indians could ride down out of the hills and take the island with only a minimum of resistance. He wasn't sure he could hold his rifle steady enough to hit a target more than a few feet away.

It was while he was contemplating this that the cry of "Indians" echoed over the island again. Wade quickly gripped his rifle and wheeled to face the south, from which the cry indicated the Indians were coming.

He could fight yet, and he would.

He saw them coming down the hill over half a mile away. He blinked, wondering if his weakness was causing his eyes to play tricks on him. For he saw what looked like a wagon. The riders far out in front didn't ride like Indians, and they certainly weren't coming in a line in an organized charge.

Then he knew. That wagon was an ambulance. And those front riders were soldiers, not Indians. Others on the island made the discovery about the same time as Wade did. Hoarse yells from weak throats went up as men climbed out of their pits to wave their hats and rifles at the column coming toward them.

The soldiers hit the river and rode on to the north, where the Indians left the hills in wild disorder, proof that there weren't enough of them left there to put up a fight against a troop of organized cavalry.

The next hour was like a hazy dream to Wade. He felt more like a spectator standing back and watching than a participant in the excitement of the rescue. His relief was so great that his knees threatened to give way.

"It was Donovan who got through," Sloan said as he and Wade rested in the grass along the river bank; "not Stillwell and Trudeau."

"They didn't make it?"

"I guess they made it, too. But Donovan got back here first. That's what counts. If he hadn't made it to-day, they redskins might have decided to take over. They could have done it any time, you know."

Wade nodded. He knew, all right. "Were those colored troops at Ft. Wallace?"

"I heard Donovan telling Colonel Forsyth that he found Colonel Carpenter and his troop out on patrol south of here."

The command was moved some distance from the

island, where the air was free of the stench of rotting horseflesh, and each man was given a little to eat. The army doctor worked on the wounds of the survivors. Only one man, Louis Farley, died after the doctor got to work. Farley's leg was amputated, but the poison from the wound had spread too far through his body.

Wade thought he had never enjoyed a supper more than he did the hardtack, beans, and hot coffee given him by the cook of the colored company. For the first night in a week and a half Wade rested peacefully.

The next day Stillwell arrived with Col. Bankhead and his troop from Ft. Wallace. He had come straight north from the fort to the Republican and followed the river down to the island, believing that ambulances couldn't make it straight across the hills. Donovan had known he hadn't time to make the detour and had tried the short cut in spite of warnings, making it successfully.

With two companies of soldiers to escort them home, Wade couldn't help thinking what so large an army could have done against the foe ten days before.

Care of the wounded and rest for all the survivors delayed them two more days before the start for Ft. Wallace. Even then it wasn't a fast trip. Speed no longer was important. The first night away from the Arickaree found them camping on the south fork of the Republican River. There they came on four Indians who were guarding a burial ground. The Indians fled, and Wade was among those who inspected the burial ground. Most of the Indians had been wrapped in their blankets with their possessions and laid on stands set on poles several feet above the ground.

"To keep the coyote away," Sloan said. "Coyotes will dig but they can't climb."

While the caravan of ambulances and the two companies of mounted soldiers moved slowly toward Ft. Wallace, Wade began to fret. No one else was in any hurry, but time was running out for him.

Wade supposed Dack was still in complete command back in Paradise. There was no way of freeing his mind of the threat Ardy had made that night there by the island. Obviously it had been intended to cut Wade to the quick and throw him off guard, but Wade didn't doubt that Ardy had been telling the truth.

Dack was the kind of man to think he could have any and all the women he desired. He had told Wade once that Martha was to be Spurlock's. But Wade knew that any time Dack himself wanted her, he would have expected Spurlock to step aside.

Now that Spurlock was dead, Dack would assume possession of Martha just as he would of a horse a friend had left.

As for Jennie, she would probably marry Dack before she learned the truth about the man. Wade carried the proof that would convince her right in his pocket. But what good was it going to do while he was out here on the Kansas-Colorado border? If only the caravan would hurry!

It was a grand welcome they got at Ft. Wallace. When the story of their heroic stand was told, there was nothing too good for any of Forsyth's men. But the one thing Wade wanted most was something nobody at Ft. Wallace could give him. He had to know that both Jennie and Martha were safe from Herman Dack.

XX

Wade waited only until the morning after his arrival at Ft. Wallace to hand in his resignation from Col. Forsyth's scouts. He tried to get Red Sloan to do the same.

"The job isn't done yet," Sloan said.

"We've done our part."

Sloan nodded. "Maybe so. But we got only a few of that bunch, remember. There's an awful lot we didn't touch."

"And you figure on getting them all single-handed, I suppose."

Sloan grinned. "Hardly. But I hear rumors here at the fort that there is going to be a winter campaign to go right down into Oklahoma and Texas after those varmints. They've been coming up here each summer, killing and stealing, then going back down there to get fat during the winter, figuring we won't bother them there. That ought to be a good time to teach them a real lesson."

"And you want to be in on it?"

Sloan shrugged. "You know me. I like excitement."

"I've had enough for a while," Wade said. But even as he said it, he was wondering about Dack. Until Dack was accounted for, his battle wasn't over.

"How about Jennie?" Wade asked after a moment.

For the first time, a frown flitted across Sloan's face. "I sure wish I could see her. But I've got to be sure this frontier is going to be a safe place for her and others like her to live in. Then I'll have something important to say to her."

"Can I tell her you'll be coming back?"

"No later than next spring," Sloan said. "If this winter campaign comes off, I aim to be in it. After that, whether we win or lose, I'll be back. Tell Jennie that."

"I'll do that," Wade said, and held out his hand. Sloan gripped it firmly.

Wade caught the first train from Sheridan and rode it all the way to Ellsworth, just a few miles from Ft. Harker. There he bought a horse.

The main topic of conversation in Ellsworth was the stand made by Forsyth's men, although it was well over two hundred miles from the island in the shallow Arickaree on the Colorado plains. The news had come in on the telegraph earlier but was just now being printed in the papers.

"Boy, you look like you had been pulled through a knothole backwards," the livery man said as Wade paid for his horse.

"Been traveling a long time," Wade said, impatient to be on his way.

The livery man sized up Wade's hollow frame. He was fifteen pounds below his normal weight, and his clothes hung on him like rags on a scarecrow.

"You look like you'd had a rough time," the livery man said. "But can you imagine how Forsyth's men must look after starving for nine days with those murdering Indians only twenty feet away, shooting at them every time they lifted their head an inch to drink a drop of water? Those men were really brave."

"Maybe the Indians weren't that close," Wade said, tightening the cinch on his saddle.

"Oh, yes, they were. I heard direct from a fellow who knew. Forsyth's men threw up sand barriers, and the Indians got right on the other side. They were afraid to climb over the barricades, for Forsyth's men were real scrappers. So they just waited and picked off every one that raised a finger. You can't imagine what torment that was for them."

"Maybe I can," Wade said, swinging into the saddle.

"Ha!" the man exclaimed. "Just because you lost a few pounds riding around, you think you've had it rough. Think of Forsyth's men. You ain't got no cause to complain."

"I'm not complaining."

Wade nudged his horse down the street, heading out of town to the north. He guessed from the talk that the town had heard about Forsyth's stand a couple of days before. If the people of Paradise had stayed in Minneapolis to await good news of the Indian fighting before returning to Paradise, they should have heard it by now. Probably they were already back in Paradise. Indian scare or not, Wade couldn't imagine the people staying away from their homes any longer.

With each mile the horse traveled, the tension in Wade grew.

He came into the valley a half-mile west of town and reined to the east toward the single street. The October sun was sinking behind him. In its slanting light, Wade studied the deserted street.

He had guessed wrong. The inhabitants of Paradise had not returned. Apparently the town had been deserted since he had left almost two months before.

Disappointment washed over him. He had thought he had come to the end of the trail. His nerves, his body and his mind had been keyed for the showdown with Dack. Now it had to be postponed. He could feel every fiber of his being unwinding as his horse reached the end of the street and passed the house where he and Solly had lived through most of the summer.

Now he would have to ride on in search of Dack.

He had reached the corner of the corral that enclosed the lot west of the livery barn when something slammed against his arm, jerking it back and knocking him off balance.

Half from the force of the blow, half from instinct, Wade slid out of the saddle, conscious of the sharp report of a rifle echoing in the empty street. As he hit the ground at the corner of the corral, it flashed through his mind that Dack was there. He had been there, waiting for him.

The horse bolted up the street, and Wade rolled

under the lowest pole of the corral fence. He lay flat for a moment, trying to gather his shattered wits. It was his left arm that was hit. Blood was pouring out onto his shirt sleeve. The arm was numb; he didn't know whether the bone had been broken or not.

He reached for his gun in its holster and breathed easier when he found it still there. His rifle had gone on down the street with his horse.

The rifleman up the street snapped shots into the corral close to Wade, but none found its target. The grass had grown up on both sides of the pole fence in the two months that no horses had been there to nibble it off, and now it gave good protection to Wade.

Wade discovered that the shots were coming from the corner of the blacksmith shop across the street. That could account for his being alive, he realized. The rifleman had been looking almost directly into the sun when he had fired. With Wade making such a big target, he had evidently felt he couldn't miss, in spite of the handicap of having the sun in his eyes.

Now Wade had to do something to bring the rifleman out in the open where he could get at him with his .45. But first he had to get closer himself. If the rifleman should step out into the street in front of the blacksmith shop right now, Wade probably wouldn't be able to hit him. The range was too great for accuracy.

Wriggling forward, dragging his wounded arm, Wade moved along the corral fence, depending on the grass to hide his movements. He reasoned that his attacker had to be Dack with the rifle. Like everyone else in the country, he must have heard of Forsyth's stand on the Arickaree. And Wade had written to Jennie the day he and Sloan had decided to join Forsyth's scouts.

Dack would have learned from Jennie that Wade was with Forsyth. When news of the escape of Forsyth's scouts came over the telegraph wire, Dack realized that Wade would make a beeline for Paradise if he was able. So he had come there hoping, if Wade did show up, to eliminate him. No one would ever know just where between Ft. Wallace and Paradise he had disappeared. Then Dack would have nothing between him and the goal he had set for himself.

Wade's arm was still numb as he inched along toward the corner of the barn. He didn't underestimate the fight ahead of him. Dack had failed in his ambush attempt. He was faced with an actual battle now, but the odds were still all on his side.

When Wade was just a few feet from the barn, the

rifle opened up again with three rapid shots. Somehow the rifleman had spotted Wade's movements. Those shots hadn't been wild wasted ones. They had all come close, one nicking through Wade's pants leg and breaking the skin.

Wade leaped up and lunged for the protection of the barn, making it without being hit again. He dived through the side door and, in the semi-darkness of the interior, made his way to the front.

Most of Dack's advantage was gone now. From Wade's vantage point at the edge of the barn door, he could see the corner of the blacksmith shop. Dack was gone.

Then suddenly a rifle bullet cut through the wood just inches from Wade's head. Wade dropped into the dried litter on the barn floor and lay quiet as rifle bullets methodically cut a pattern along the side of the door. Either Dack had seen him there or had guessed he would come there. If that first shot had been a little to the right or if Wade had stayed on his feet, the fight would have been over now.

For a long time after the last shot ripped into the barn, Wade didn't move. Then he raised himself on his good elbow and peeked out the door. Dack was nowhere in sight. Wade guessed the shots had come from the doorway of the blacksmith shop.

He raised himself to a crouch but didn't use his gun. As yet he hadn't fired a shot. Maybe if he kept quiet Dack would think his shots had found their mark. Dack would have to make sure. He couldn't leave Wade's body for others to find. It was the only chance Wade had against Dack's rifle. So Wade made no move. It was certain either he or Dack was not going to leave the town alive.

Then Dack abruptly burst from the door of the blacksmith shop, running toward the corner of the barn. Wade could have cut him down. Dack hadn't given him even that much of a chance. But Wade had never deliberately killed a man who wasn't shooting at him. He couldn't now.

Stepping quickly out of the doorway, he called sharply, "Dack!"

Dack stopped as though already hit by a bullet—but only for a moment. He brought the rifle around, throwing himself to the ground in a long roll as he fired.

Wade felt the breath of the bullet as it snapped past his head. Then his own gun was bucking in his hand.

No dust spurted up in the street from his shot. Wade knew he hadn't missed.

After it was over, the lonely street seemed to echo from those last shots. Then complete silence closed in. Slowly Wade turned up the street toward his father's store. Now that the showdown had come and he had won, he felt sick.

The numbness was leaving his arm, and pain was beginning to burn through it. There should be something in his father's store that he could use to ease the pain and bandage the arm until he could ride to Minneapolis.

But before he got to the store, a lone rider came down the bluff from the northeast, riding hard. Wade stopped. Surely it couldn't be more trouble. Dack had marked the end of violence for him.

Then he realized a woman was on the horse. And a moment later he recognized Martha. She wheeled her horse into the street and stopped a few feet from Wade. Before he realized what she was going to do, she had slid from the horse and run to him, throwing her arms around him.

Instantly she drew back, looking at her right hand and the sleeve of her dress where Wade's blood was a bright crimson in the rays of the setting sun.

"You're hurt, Wade," she breathed, the joy of a moment before gone from her face. "How bad?"

"Not bad, Martha," Wade said.

"Those shots I heard—I thought it might be you. That's why I came on ahead. What happened?"

"Dack was waiting for me. I had to do it, Martha. He gave me no choice."

Wade watched her face. She just had to understand.

"I know, Wade. I know now what kind of man Herman Dack was."

"Did he ever lay a hand on you?"

"He tried. I used a whip on him. I'm glad he's dead."

"How do Jennie and Dad feel?"

"They saw through Dack, too, especially Jennie."

"I brought back proof of the kind of man he was," Wade said, feeling for the ring in his pocket.

"That will kill any doubt that is left, I know. Now let's go to the store. I'll fix your arm."

"The others coming?" Wade asked as they moved down the street.

"Everybody. We heard about your fight on the Arickaree. We felt that that fight made it safe for us to come back. They'll all be here tonight." She looked up into his gaunt face. "I knew you'd come back here as soon as you could. Was the fight terrible?"

"Bad enough. But that's all behind me now. I want to forget violence. I want to live the way you like, if you'll have me now, Martha."

They were on the porch of the store, and Martha stopped. "I learned a lot of things in Minneapolis, Wade. I attended the funeral of some people who were killed by the Indians. I heard stories of how people had to live and fight. It's a violent country, and it takes strong men to live in it. I don't want you to change, Wade. I want a strong man."

Wade had never felt stronger than he did at that moment as he used his good arm to press Martha to him.

"We must dress that arm," Martha said.

"Let it wait just a minute. A strong man wants a kiss and a promise."

He got them both.

ANDREW J. FENADY

Owen Wister Award-Winning Author of *Big Ike*

No mission is too dangerous as long as the cause—
and the money—are right. Four soldiers of fortune,
along with a beautiful woman, have crossed the
Mexican border to dig up five million dollars in
buried gold. But between the Trespassers and their
treasure lie a merciless comanchero guerilla band,
a tribe of hostile Yaqui Indians and Benito Juarez's
army. It's a journey no one with any sense would
hope to survive, or would even dare to try, except...

The Trespassers

Andrew J. Fenady is a Spur Award finalist and re-
cipient of the prestigious Owen Wister Award for
his lifelong contribution to Western literature, and
the Golden Boot Award, in recognition of his contri-
butions to the Western genre. He has written eleven
novels and numerous screenplays, including the
classic John Wayne film *Chisum*.

AVAILABLE MAY 2008!

ISBN 13: 978-0-8439-6024-2

☐ YES!

Sign me up for the Leisure Western Book Club and send my FREE BOOKS! If I choose to stay in the club, I will pay only $14.00* each month, a savings of $9.96!

NAME: _____

ADDRESS: _____

TELEPHONE: _____

EMAIL: _____

☐ I want to pay by credit card.

☐ VISA   ☐ MasterCard   ☐ DISCOVER

ACCOUNT #: _____

EXPIRATION DATE: _____

SIGNATURE: _____

Mail this page along with $2.00 shipping and handling to:
Leisure Western Book Club
PO Box 6640
Wayne, PA 19087
Or fax (must include credit card information) to:
610-995-9274

You can also sign up online at **www.dorchesterpub.com**.

*Plus $2.00 for shipping. Offer open to residents of the U.S. and Canada only. Canadian residents please call 1-800-481-9191 for pricing information.

If under 18, a parent or guardian must sign. Terms, prices and conditions subject to change. Subscription subject to acceptance. Dorchester Publishing reserves the right to reject any order or cancel any subscription.